DATE DUE

NO 1 2 '03			
DE 0 4 '03			
FE 0 Z '04			
MR 0 2 '04			
MR 2 5 '04			
AP 2 < '04			
JY 1 5 '04			
AG 1 3 '04			
SE 2 2 '04			
JA 2 5 '05			
AP 1 0 '05			
APR 2 0 2010			

Hammond came over and took and kissed the hand which Maggie had suddenly thrown at her side. "We both owe everything to Priscilla," he said.

Priscilla's Promise

Priscilla's Promise

L. T. Meade

EDITED BY
Heather Harpham Kopp

HARVEST HOUSE PUBLISHERS
Eugene, Oregon 97402

101303

Cover by Koechel Peterson and Associates, Minneapolis, Minnesota.

Interior illustrations by Joneile Emery, derived from original illustrations from the Victorian period.

PRISCILLA'S PROMISE

Copyright © 1998 by Harvest House Publishers
Eugene, Oregon 97402

Library of Congress Cataloging-in-Publication Data

Meade, L.T., 1854–1914.
    Priscilla's promise   L.T. Meade.
        p.   cm.   —   (Victorian bookshelf series)
    Updated ed. of: A sweet girl graduate. c1910.
    Edited by Heather Harpham Kopp.
    ISBN 1-56507-855-1
    I. Kopp, Heather Harpham, 1964–   . II. Meade, L.T., 1854-1914.
Sweet girl graduate.   III. Title.   IV. Series.
PR4990.M34P75   1998
823'.8—dc21   97-31384
                                                                              CIP

Printed in the United States of America.

98   99   00   01   02   03   / DC /   10   9   8   7   6   5   4   3   2   1

THE AFFECTION OF FRIENDS

"Go to her. She is waiting for you—
and oh, I know that her heart has been waiting for
you for a long, long time."

Afternoon tea parties, bright laughter, shared dreams. . . gossip, conspiracies, and jealous outbursts.

Welcome to the world of St. Benet's college for women, located in England at the turn of the century. Will the prim and earnest Priscilla Peel ever fit into the university society scene? Will the moody but beguiling Maggie Oliphant ever admit that she is in love with Mr. Hammond? And what is the mystery behind the death of the adorable Annabel Lee?. . . .

For decades women have been rescuing beautiful old books like *Priscilla's Promise* from dusty shelves or attics. Laid invitingly on an end table, these antique keepsakes lend a touch of Victorian charm to any room. But between their gorgeous covers, many of them also contain captivating stories to rival the most popular present-day novels.

The Victorian Bookshelf series is bringing back the best of such books. Because the authors actually lived in the time they depict, the stories reward us with delightful authenticity. And though slightly condensed, details of period charm—including language, dress, and setting—have been preserved whenever possible.

Priscilla's Promise was originally published around 1892 as *A Sweet Girl Graduate*. The author, Elizabeth Thomasina Smith, known as L.T. Meade, wrote more than 250 books in her lifetime, including children's books, mysteries, and many popular "books for girls." The daughter of a minister father, her faith is invariably reflected in her novels.

At the time of *Priscilla's Promise*, skepticism still abounded in England about the appropriateness of higher education for women. Our heroine, however, is determined to attend college so that she can eventually support herself and her three younger sisters.

Though academically bright, Prissie is ill-prepared for the social whirlwind. When she unwittingly incites the tempers of certain young ladies, a spiteful plan to drum her out of the college is set in motion. "Horrid minx!" declares one girl to another, "Flaunting her poverty in our very faces and refusing to make herself pleasant or one with us in any way. We must nip this growing mischief in the bud."

Soon enough, poor Prissie has been falsely accused of theft, as well as trying to flirt with the man her best friend loves. As Prissie struggles to redeem her reputation and prove her loyalty to Maggie, she forever endears herself to the reader's heart. Along the way, we savor our glimpses into the sweet affections, rituals, and complexities that have always characterized the close relationships of women.

Readers will also appreciate the occasional passages excerpted throughout the novel from popular etiquette books of the day, such as *Etiquette for Ladies and Gentleman* (1877), *The Modern Hostess* (1904), and *The Book of Good Manners* (1923). We can't help smiling when we read tips such as, "When the hair is harsh, poor, and dry, nothing lubricates better than pure unscented salad oil."

Life has changed so much in a hundred years! But with just the turn of a page, antique romances such as the one you're holding offer a delightful opportunity to revisit the past and recapture some of its charm.

—*Heather Harpham Kopp*

Going Out
into the World

riscilla's trunk was neatly packed. It was a new trunk and had a nice canvas covering over it. The canvas was bound with red braid, and Priscilla's initials were worked on the top in large, plain letters. Her initials were P.P.P., and they stood for Priscilla Penywern Peel. The trunk was corded and strapped and put away, and Priscilla stood by her aunt's side in the little parlor of Penywern Cottage.

"Well, I think I've told you everything," said the aunt.

"Oh, yes, Aunt Ruby, I shan't forget. I'm to write once a week, and I'm to try not to be nervous. I don't suppose I shall be—I don't see why I should. Girls aren't nervous nowadays, are they?"

"I don't know, my dear. It seems to me that if they aren't they ought to be. I can understand girls doing hard things if they must. I can understand anyone doing anything that has to be done, but as to not being nervous—well—there! Sit down, Prissie, child, and take your tea."

Priscilla was tall and slight. Her figure was younger than her years, which were nearly nineteen, but her face was much older.

7

It was an almost careworn face, thoughtful, grave, with anxious lines already deepening the seriousness of the too-serious mouth.

Priscilla cut some bread and butter and poured out some tea for her aunt and for herself.

Miss Ruby Peel was not the least like her niece. She was short and rather dumpy. She had a sensible, downright sort of face.

"Well, I'm tired," she said, when the meal was over. "I think I'll go to bed early. We have said all our last words, haven't we, Priscilla?"

"Pretty nearly, Aunt Ruby."

"Oh, yes, that reminds me—there's one thing more. Your fees will be all right, of course, and your traveling, and I have arranged about your washing money."

"Yes Aunt Ruby, everything is all right."

Priscilla fidgeted, moved her position a little, and looked longingly out of the window.

"You must have a little money over and above these things," proceeded Aunt Ruby.

"I don't hold with the present craze about women's education. But I feel somehow that I shall be proud of you."

Aunt Ruby continued in her sedate voice. "I am not rich, but I'll allow you—yes, I'll manage to allow you two shillings a week. That will be for pocket money, you understand, child."

The girl's face flushed painfully.

"I'll want a few pence for stamps, of course," she said. "But I shan't write a great many letters. I'll be a great deal too busy studying. You need not allow me anything like so large a sum as that, Aunt Ruby."

"Nonsense, child. You'll find it all too small when you go out into the world. You are a clever girl, Prissie, and I'm going to be proud of you. Yes, I'll make it ten shillings a month—yes, I will. I can easily scrape that sum out of the butter money. Now, not another word. I'm off to bed. Good night, my love."

Priscilla kissed her aunt and went out. It was a lovely autumn evening. She stepped onto the green lawn which surrounded the little cottage, and with the moonlight casting its full radiance on her slim figure, looked steadily out over the sea. The cottage was on the top of some high cliffs. The light of the moon made a bright path over the water, and Priscilla had a good view of shining, silvered water and dark, deep blue sky.

She stood perfectly still, gazing straight out before her. Some of the reflection and brightness of the moonlight seemed to get into her anxious eyes and the faint dawn of a newly-born hope trembled around her lips. She thought herself rich with ten shillings a month of pocket money. She returned to the house, feeling overwhelmed by Aunt Ruby's goodness.

Upstairs in Prissie's room there were two beds. One was small; in this she herself slept. The other now had three occupants. Three heads were raised when Prissie entered the room and three shrill voices exclaimed:

"Here we are, all wide awake, Prissie, darling!"

This remark, made simultaneously, was followed by prolonged peals of laughter.

"Three of you in that small bed!" said Priscilla.

She stood still, and a smile broke all over her face. "Why, Hattie," she said, catching up the eldest of the three girls and giving her a fervent hug, "how did you slip out of Aunt Ruby's room?"

"Oh, I managed to," said Hattie in a stage whisper. "Aunt Ruby came upstairs half an hour ago, and she undressed very fast, and got into bed, and I heard her snoring in about a minute. It was then I slipped away. She never heard."

"Hop up on the bed now, Prissie," exclaimed Rose, another of the children, "and let us all have a chat. Here, Katie, if you'll promise not to cry, you may get into the middle, between Hattie and me."

Katie was the youngest of the three occupants of the bed; she was eight years old, and self-control could scarcely be expected of her.

Priscilla placed her candle on the mantelpiece, jumped on the bed according to orders, and looked earnestly at her three small sisters.

"Now, Prissie," said Hattie in the important little voice that she always used, "begin, go on—tell us all about your grand college life."

"How can I, Hattie, when I don't know what to say? I can't *guess* what I am to do at college."

"Oh, dear," sighed Rose, "I only wish I were the one to go! It will be very dull living with Aunt Ruby when you are away, Priscilla. She won't let us take long walks, and if ever we go in for a real jolly lark we are sure to be punished."

"Even though it is for your good, I wish with all my heart you were not going away, Prissie," said Hattie in her blunt fashion.

Priscilla colored. Then she spoke with firmness. "We have had enough of this kind of talk. Katie, you shall come and sit in my lap, darling. I'll wrap you up quite warm in this big shawl. Now, girls," she said, "what *is* the use of making things harder? You know, perfectly, you two elder ones, why I must go away, and you, Katie, you know also, don't you?"

"Yes, Prissie," answered Katie, speaking in a broken, half-sobbing voice, "only I *am* so lonely."

"By and by I'll come back to you all. Once every year, at least, I'll come back. And then, after I've gone through my course of study, I'll get work of some sort—a good, steady job—and you three shall come and live with me. There, what do you say to that? Only three years, and then such a jolly time. Why, Katie will be only eleven then!"

Priscilla spoke in a remarkably cheerful voice, but the three little sisters who were to stay behind with Aunt Ruby still viewed things dismally.

"If Aunt Ruby wasn't just what she is—" began Hattie.

"If she didn't think the least tiny morsel of a lark wrong—" continued Rose.

"Why, then we could pull along somehow," sighed Hattie.

"Oh, you'll pull along as it is," said Priscilla. "I'll write to you as often as ever I can. If possible, I'll keep a sort of journal and send it to you. And perhaps there'll be stories with larks in them. Now you really must go to sleep, for I have to get up so early in the morning. Katie, darling, I'll make a corner for you in my bed tonight. Won't that be a treat?"

"Oh, yes, Prissie."

Katie's pale face was lit up by a radiant smile; Hattie and Rose lay down side by side and closed their eyes. In a few moments they were sound asleep.

Priscilla bent over them and kissed them. Then, before she lay down herself, she knelt by the window, looked up at the clear, dark sky in which the moon sailed in majesty, bent her head, murmured a few words of prayer, then crept into bed by her little sister's side.

Prissie felt full of courage and good resolves. She was going out into the world tomorrow, and she was quite determined that the world should not conquer her, although she knew that she was a very poor maiden with a specially heavy load of care on her young shoulders.

᚛II᚜

The Delights
of Being a Fresher

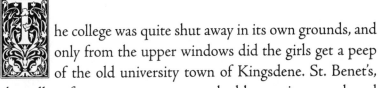he college was quite shut away in its own grounds, and only from the upper windows did the girls get a peep of the old university town of Kingsdene. St. Benet's, the college for women, was approached by a private road, and high entrance gates obstructed the gaze of the curious. Inside there were cheerful halls and pleasant gardens and gay, fresh, unrestrained life. But the passer-by got no peep of these things unless the high gates happened to be open.

This was the first evening of term, and most of the girls were back. There was nothing very particular going on, and they were walking about the gardens, greeting old friends, and more or less picking up the threads which had been broken or loosened in the long vacation.

The evenings were getting shorter, but the pleasant twilight that was soon to be rendered brilliant by the full moon seemed to the girls even nicer to linger about in than broad daylight. They did not want to go into the houses; they flitted about in groups here and there, chatting and laughing merrily.

13

St. Benet's had three halls, each with its own vice-principal, and a certain number of resident students. Each hall stood on its own grounds and was more or less a complete home in itself. There were resident lecturers for the whole college and one lady principal who took the lead.

Miss Vincent was the name of the present principal. She was an old lady and had a vice-principal under her at Vincent Hall, the largest and newest of these spacious homes, where young women received the advantages of university instruction to prepare them for the battles of life.

Priscilla was to live at Heath Hall—a slightly smaller house, which stood at a little distance away—its grounds being divided from the grounds of Vincent Hall by means of a rustic wooden fence. Miss Heath was the very popular vice-principal of this hall, and Prissie was considered a fortunate girl to obtain a home in her house. She sat now huddled up in one corner of the carriage which turned in at the wide gates, and finally deposited her and her luggage at the back entrance of Heath Hall.

Priscilla looked out in the darkness of the autumn night with frightened eyes. She hated herself for feeling nervous. She had told Aunt Ruby that of course she would have no silly tremors, yet here she was trembling and scarcely able to pay the cabman his fare.

She heard a girl's laugh, and it caused her to start so violently that she dropped one of her few treasured sixpences, which went rolling about aimlessly almost under the horse's hoofs.

"Stop a minute, I'll find it for you," said a voice. A tall girl with big brown eyes suddenly darted into view, picked up the sixpence as if by magic, popped it into Priscilla's hand, and then vanished. Priscilla heard her laughing again as she turned to join someone who was standing beside a laurel hedge. The two linked their arms together and walked off in the darkness.

"Such a frightened poor fresher!" said the girl who had picked up the sixpence.

"Maggie," said the other in a warning voice, "I know you, I know what you mean to do."

"My dear, good Nancy, it is more than I know myself. What awful indiscretion does your prophetic soul see me perpetrating?"

"Oh, Maggie, as if anything could change your nature! You know you'll take up that miserable fresher for about a fortnight, and make her imagine that you're going to be excellent friends for the rest of your life, and then—*poof!* You'll snuff her out as if she had never existed; I know you, Maggie, and I call it cruel."

"Is not that Miss Nancy Banister I hear talking?" said a voice quite close to the two girls.

They both turned and, with heightened color, immediately rushed up to shake hands with the vice-principal of their college.

"How do you do, my dears?" Miss Heath said in a hearty voice. "Are you quite well, Maggie, and you, Nancy? Did you have a pleasant holiday?"

As the girls began answering eagerly, other girls came up and joined the group, all anxious to shake hands with Miss Heath and to get a word of greeting from her.

At this moment the dressing-gong for dinner sounded, and the little group moved slowly toward the house.

In the entrance hall, many girls who had recently arrived were standing about. All had a nod, or a smile, or a kiss for Maggie Oliphant.

"How do you do, Miss Oliphant? Come and see me tonight in my room, won't you, dear?" issued from many mouths.

In her good-natured, affectionate way, Maggie promised she would.

Nancy Banister was also greeted by several friends. She, too, was gay and bright, but quieter than Maggie. Her face was more reliable in its expression, but not nearly so beautiful.

She had washed her hands, and removed her muddy boots, and smoothed out her straight, light brown hair.

"If you accept all these invitations, Maggie," Nancy said as the two girls walked down the corridor that led to their rooms, "you know you will have to sit up until morning. Why will you say 'yes' to every one? You know it only causes disappointment and jealousy."

Maggie laughed.

"My dear, good creature, don't worry your righteous soul," she answered. "I'll call on all the girls I can, and the others must grin and bear it. Now we barely have time to change our dresses for dinner. Surely, though, Nance, there's a light under Annabel Lee's door. Who have they dared to put into her room? It must be one of those wretched freshers. I don't think I can bear it. I shall have to go away into another corridor."

"Maggie, dear—you are far too sensitive. Could the college afford to keep a room empty because poor, dear Annie Lee once occupied it?"

"They could, they ought," burst from Maggie. She stamped her foot with anger. "That room is a shrine to me. It will always be a shrine. I shall hate the person who lives in it." Tears filled her bright brown eyes. Her arched, proud lips trembled. She opened her door and, going into her room, shut it with a bang, almost in Nancy's face.

Nancy stood still for a moment. A quick sigh escaped from her lips.

"Maggie is the dearest girl in the college," she said to herself; "the dearest, the sweetest, the prettiest, yet also the most provoking. It is the greatest wonder she has kept so long out of some serious scrape. She will never leave here without doing something outrageous, and yet there isn't a girl in the place as loved as her. I wish…" here Nancy sighed again and put her hand to her brow as if to chase away some perplexity. Then, after a moment's hesitation, she went up to the door of the room next to Maggie's and knocked.

There was a moment's silence, then a tight, thin voice said, "Come in."

Nancy entered at once.

Priscilla Peel was standing in the center of the room. The electric light was turned on, revealing the bareness and absence of all ornament of the apartment; a fire was laid in the grate but not lit, and Priscilla's ugly square trunk, its canvas covering removed, stood in the center of the floor. Priscilla had taken off her jacket and hat. She had washed her hands, removed her muddy boots, and smoothed out her straight, light brown hair. She looked what she felt—a very stiff and unformed specimen of girlhood. There was a great lump in her throat, brought there by mingled nervousness and home-sickness, but that very fact only made her manner icy and repellent.

"Forgive me," said Nancy, blushing all over her rosy face. "I thought perhaps you might like to know one or two things, as you are new here. My name is Nancy Banister. I have a room in the same corridor, but quite at the other end. You must come and visit me presently. Oh, has no one lit your fire? Wouldn't you like one? The evenings are turning so chilly now, and a fire in one's room gives one a homelike feeling, doesn't it? Shall I light it for you?"

"No, no, thank you," said Priscilla stiffly. She longed to rush at Nancy and smother her with kisses, but she could only stand in the middle of her room, helpless and awkward, held in a terrible bondage of shyness.

"Don't I just loathe myself! How hideously I do my hair, and what a frightful dress I have on. Oh, I wish I were at home again."

Nancy drew back a step, chilled in spite of herself.

"I see there are matches on the mantel," she said, "so you can light the fire yourself whenever you like. The gong that will sound in a minute will be for dinner, and Miss Heath always likes us to be punctual for that meal. It does not matter about any other. Do you think you can find your way to the dining hall, or shall I come and fetch you?"

"No—thank you. I—I can manage."

"But I'll come with pleasure if you'd like me to."

"No, I'd rather you didn't trouble, please."

"Very well, if you're sure you know the way. You go down the broad stairs, then turn to the right, then to the left. Good-bye. I must rush off, or I shall be late."

Nancy shut the door behind her. She did it gently, although she did not feel gentle, for she had a distinct sensation of being irritated.

Meanwhile Priscilla, clasping her hands together behind the closed door, looked yearningly in the direction where the bright face and trim, neat girlish figure had stood. She was trembling slightly and her eyes slowly filled with tears.

"I feel sick and lonely and horrid," she said under her breath. "Talk of nerves; oh, if Aunt Ruby could see me now! Why, I'm positively shaking. What would the children say if they saw their Prissie now? And I'm the girl who is to fight the world and kill the dragon and make a home for the nestlings. Don't I feel like it! Don't I look like it! Don't I just loathe myself! How hideously I do my hair, and what a frightful dress I have on. Oh, I wish I were at home again."

Crash! bang! pealed the great gong through the house. Doors opened all along the corridor, and light steps passed Priscilla's room. She heard the rustle of silk and the sweet, high tinkle of girlish laughter.

She stayed in her room till the last footsteps had died away, then in desperation made a rush for it, flew down the wide stairs in a bashful agony, and, as a matter of course, entered the spacious dining hall by the door devoted to the teachers.

A girl's life at one of the women's colleges is supposed to be more or less an unfettered sort of existence. The broad rules guiding conduct are little more than those that must be exercised in any well-organized family. But there is the unspoken etiquette made chiefly by the students themselves, which can only be transgressed at the risk of sharp glances, muttered comments, and even words of derision.

No student was expected to enter the hall by the teacher's entrance, and for this enormity to be perpetrated by a fresher immediately made her the subject of all eyes. Poor Priscilla was unconscious of any offense. She grew scarlet under the gaze of the merciless stares and further added to her sins by sitting down at one of the tables at the top of the hall.

No one reproved her in words or requested her to take a lower seat, but some rude giggles were heard; and Priscilla, who would thankfully have taken her dinner in the scullery, heard hints about a certain young person's presumption, and about the cheek of those wretched freshers, which must instantly be put down with a high hand.

Priscilla had choked over her soup and was making poor headway with the fish that followed when suddenly a sweet, low voice addressed her.

"This is your first evening at St. Benet's," said the voice. "I hope you will be happy. I know you will, after a little."

Priscilla turned and met the full gaze of lovely eyes, brown like a nut, soft and deep as the thick pile of velvet, and yet with a latent flash and glow in them that gave them a red, half-wild gleam every now and then. The lips that belonged to this face were slightly parted in a smile, and the expression in the eyes stole straight down with a glow of delicious comfort into Priscilla's heart.

"Thank you," she said in her stiff, wooden tone, and the girl began to talk again.

"I believe my room is next to yours. My name is Oliphant—Margaret Oliphant, but everyone calls me Maggie. That is, of course, I mean my friends do. Would you like to come into my room and let me tell you some of the rules?"

"Thank you," said Priscilla again. She longed to add, "I should love beyond words to come into your room," but instead she remarked icily, "I think Miss Heath has given me printed rules."

"Oh, you have seen our dear Dorothea—I mean Miss Heath. Isn't she lovely?"

"I don't know," answered Priscilla.

"My dear Miss—I have not caught your name—I won't say any more. You must find out for yourself. But now, about the rules, I don't mean the *printed* rules. We have, I assure you, all kinds of little etiquettes at St. Benet's that we expect each other to observe. We are supposed to be democratic and inclined to go in for all that is advanced in womanhood. But, oh dear! Let any student dare to break one of our own little rules, and she—"

"Have I broken any of them?" asked Priscilla in alarm. "I did notice that everyone stared at me when I came into the hall, but I thought it was because my face was fresh, and I hoped people would get accustomed to me by and by."

"You poor, dear child, there are lots of fresh faces here besides yours."

"But what have I done? Do tell me. I'd much rather know."

"Well, dear, you have *only* come into the hall by the teachers' entrance, and you have *only* seated yourself at the top of the table, where the learned students who are going for a B.A. with honors take their meals. That is pretty good for a fresher. Forgive me, we call the new girls freshers for a week or two. Oh, you have done nothing wrong. Of course not, how could you know any better? Only I think it would be nice for me to explain our little rules, would it not?"

"I should be very obliged," said Priscilla. "And please tell me now where I ought to sit at dinner."

Miss Oliphant's merry eyes twinkled.

"Look down this long hall," she said. "Observe that door at the further end—that is the students' door; through that door you ought to have entered."

"But please tell me where I ought to have seated myself."

"There is a table near that lower entrance, Miss—"

"Peel," interposed Priscilla. "My name is Priscilla Peel."

"How quaint and great-grandmotherly. Quite delicious! Well, Miss Peel, by that entrance door is a table, a table rather in a draught, and consecrated to the freshers—there the freshers humbly partake of nourishment."

"I see. Then I am as far from the right place as I can be."

"About as far as you can be."

"And that is why all the girls have stared so at me."

"Yes, of course."

Priscilla sat silent for a few moments. One of the neat waiting-maids removed her plate; her almost untasted dinner still lay upon it. Miss Oliphant turned to attack some roast mutton with truly British vigor.

By and by Priscilla's voice, stiff but with a break in it, fell upon her ear.

"I think the students at St. Benet's must be very cruel."

"My dear Miss Peel, the honor of the most fascinating college in England is questioned. Unsay those words."

Maggie Oliphant was joking. Her voice was gay, her eyes filled with laughter. But Priscilla, unaccustomed to light repartee or humor in any form, replied to her with heavy and pained seriousness.

"I think the students here are cruel," she repeated. "How can a stranger know which is the teachers' entrance and which is the right seat to take at table? If nobody shows her, how can a stranger know? I do think the students are cruel, and I am sorry—very sorry I came."

"At Home"

ost of the girls who sat at those dinner tables had fringed or tousled or curled locks. Priscilla's were brushed simply away from her broad forehead. After saying her last words, she bent her head low over her plate and longed even for the protection of a fringe to hide her burning blushes. Her momentary courage had evaporated; she was shocked at having betrayed herself to a stranger. Blinding tears rushed to her eyes, and her terror was that they would drop onto her plate. Suppose some of those horrid girls saw her crying? Hateful thought. She would rather die than show emotion before them.

At this moment a soft hand was slipped into hers and Maggie's voice said:

"I am so sorry anything has seemed unkind to you. Believe me, we are not what you imagine. We have our fun and our prejudices, of course, but we are not what you think we are."

Priscilla could not help smiling, nor could she resist slightly squeezing the fingers which touched hers.

"You are not unkind, I know," she answered; and she ate the rest of her dinner in a comforted frame of mind.

After dinner one of the lecturers who resided at Heath Hall, a pleasant, bright girl of two- or three-and-twenty, came and introduced herself, and presently took Priscilla with her to her own room to talk over the line of study that the young girl proposed to take up. This conference lasted some little time, and then Priscilla, in the lecturer's company, returned to the hall for tea.

A great many girls kept coming in and out. Some stayed to have tea, but most helped themselves to tea and bread and butter and took them away to their own private rooms.

Maggie Oliphant and Nancy Banister presently rushed in for this purpose. Maggie, seeing Priscilla, ran up to her.

"How are you getting on?" she asked brightly. "Oh, by-the-by, will you cocoa with me tonight at half past ten?"

"I don't know what you mean," answered Priscilla. "But I'll do it," she added, her eyes brightening.

"All right, I'll explain the simple ceremony when you come. My room is next to yours, so you'll have no difficulty in finding me out. I don't expect to have anyone present except Miss Banister," she said, nodding her head in Nancy's direction, "and perhaps one other girl. Bye-bye, I'll see you at half past ten."

Maggie turned to leave the hall, but Nancy lingered for a moment by Priscilla's side.

"Wouldn't you like to take your tea up to your room?" she asked. "We most of us do it. You may, you know."

"I don't think I wish to," answered Priscilla in an uncertain voice.

Nancy half turned to go, then came back.

"You are going to unpack by and by, aren't you?" she asked.

"Oh, yes, when I get back to my room."

"Perhaps you ought to know beforehand; the girls will be coming to call."

Priscilla raised her eyes.

"What girls?" she asked, alarm in her tone.

"Oh, most of the students in your corridor. They always call on a fresher the first night in her room. You need not bother yourself about them; they'll just talk for a little while and then go away. What is the matter, Miss Peel? Maggie has told me your name, you see."

"What you tell me sounds so very—very formal."

"But it isn't—not really. Shall I come and help you to entertain them?"

"I wish—" began Priscilla. She hesitated.

"What did you say?" Nancy bent forward a little impatiently.

"I wish—yes, do come," she said.

"All right, you may expect me."

Nancy flew after Maggie Oliphant, and Priscilla went slowly up the wide, luxurious stairs. She turned down the corridor that led to her own room. There were doors leading out of this corridor at both sides, and Priscilla caught glimpses of luxurious rooms bright with flowers and electric light. Girls were laughing and chatting in them. She noticed pictures on the walls and lounges and chairs scattered about.

Her own room was at the far end of the corridor. The electric light was also brightening it, but the fire was unlit, and the presence of the unpacked trunk gave it a very unhomelike feel. In itself, the room was particularly picturesque. It had two charming lattice windows set in deep, square bays. One window faced the fireplace, the other the door. The effect was slightly irregular, but for that very reason all the more charming. The walls of the room were painted light blue; there was a looking-glass over the mantelpiece set in a frame of the palest, most delicate blue. A picture-rail ran round the room about six feet from the ground, and above that wild roses were painted in bold, free relief.

The panels of the door were also decorated with sprays of wildflowers in picturesque confusion. Both the flowers and the wall, however, were unfinished, the final and completing touches remaining yet to be given.

Priscilla looked hungrily at these unexpected trophies of art. She could have shouted with glee as she recognized some of her dear, wild Devonshire flowers among the groups on the door panels. She wondered if all the rest of the students were treated to these artistic decorations, and she grew a little happier and less homesick at the thought.

Priscilla could have been an artist herself had the opportunity arisen, but she was one of those girls all alive with aspiration and longing who never up to the present had come in the way of special culture in any style.

She stood for some time gazing at the groups of wildflowers, then remembering with horror that she was to receive visitors that night, looked round the room to see if she could do anything to make it appear homelike and inviting.

She rushed to light the fire but could not find the matches, which had been removed from their place on the mantelpiece, and felt far too shy to ring the electric bell. It was Priscilla's fashion to clasp her hands together when she felt a sense of dismay, and she did so now as she looked around the pretty room, which yet with all its luxuries looked to her cold and dreary.

The furniture was excellent of its kind. A Turkish carpet covered the center of the floor, the boards round the edge were stained and rightly polished. In one corner of the room was a little bed, made to look like a sofa by day, with a Liberty cretonne covering. A curtain of the same fabric shut away the wardrobe and washing apparatus. Just under one of the bay windows stood a writing table, a bookcase at the top, and a chest of drawers to hold linens below. Besides this, there was a small square table for tea in the room and a couple of chairs. And yet, the whole effect was undoubtedly bare.

Priscilla was hesitating whether to begin to unpack her trunk or not when a light knock was heard at her door. She said "Come in," and two girls burst rather noisily into the apartment.

"How do you do?" they said, favoring the fresh girl with a brief nod. "You came today, didn't you? What are you going to study? Are you clever?"

These queries issued rapidly from the lips of the tallest of the girls. She had red hair tousled about her head. Her small, restless eyes now glanced at Priscilla, now wandered over the room. She did not wait for a reply to any of her questions, but turned rapidly to her companion.

"I told you so, Polly," she said. "I was quite sure that she was going to be put into Miss Lee's room. You see, I'm right. This *is* Annabel Lee's old room; it has never been occupied since."

"Hush!" said the other girl.

The two walked across the apartment and seated themselves on Priscilla's bed.

There came a fresh knock at the door, and this time three more students entered. They barely nodded to Priscilla, then rushed across the room with cries of rapture to greet the girls who were seated on the bed.

"How do you do, Miss Singleton? How do you do, Miss Jones?"

Miss Jones and Miss Singleton exchanged kisses with Miss Phillips, Miss Marsh, and Miss Day. The babel of tongues rose high, and everyone had something to say with regard to the

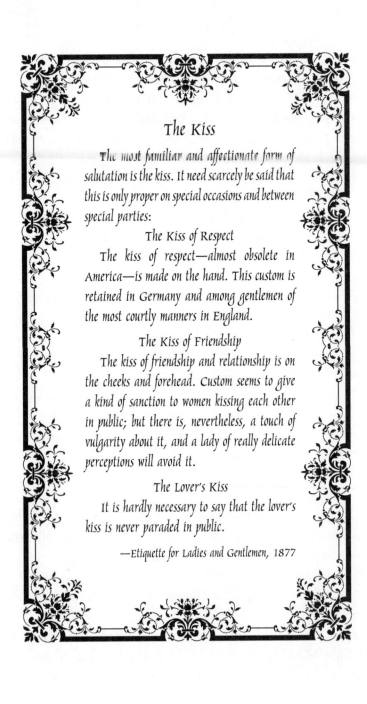

The Kiss

The most familiar and affectionate form of salutation is the kiss. It need scarcely be said that this is only proper on special occasions and between special parties:

The Kiss of Respect

The kiss of respect—almost obsolete in America—is made on the hand. This custom is retained in Germany and among gentlemen of the most courtly manners in England.

The Kiss of Friendship

The kiss of friendship and relationship is on the cheeks and forehead. Custom seems to give a kind of sanction to women kissing each other in public; but there is, nevertheless, a touch of vulgarity about it, and a lady of really delicate perceptions will avoid it.

The Lover's Kiss

It is hardly necessary to say that the lover's kiss is never paraded in public.

—Etiquette for Ladies and Gentlemen, 1877

room that had been assigned to Priscilla.

"Look," said Miss Day, "it was in that corner she had her rocking chair. Girls, *do* you remember Annabel's rocking chair, and how she used to sway herself backward and forward in it and half shut her lovely eyes?"

"Oh, and don't I just seem to *see* that little red tea table of hers near the fire," burst from Miss Marsh. "That Japanese table, with the Japanese tea set—

"When Miss Peel unpacks her trunk, she'll make the room look very pretty, too. She couldn't possibly exist in it as it is now."

oh dear, oh dear! Those cups of tea—those cakes! Well, the room *was* luxurious, *was* worth coming to see in Annabel's time."

"'Twas more than it is now," laughed Miss Jones in a harsh voice. "How bare the walls look without her pictures. It was in that recess the large figure of 'Hope' by Burne-Jones used to hang, and there, that queer, wild, wonderful head looking out of clouds. You know she never would tell us the artist's name. Yes, she had pretty things everywhere! How the room is altered! I don't think I care for it a bit now."

"Could anyone who knew Annabel Lee care for the room without her?" asked one of the girls.

"Well," said one merry little girl, who was spoken to by the others as Ada Hardy, "I have no doubt that by and by, when Miss—" She glanced toward Priscilla.

"Peel," faltered Priscilla.

"When Miss Peel unpacks her trunk, she'll make the room look very pretty, too. She couldn't possibly exist in it as it is now."

29

"I can tell you of a leading shop in Kingsdene, Miss Peel," said Miss Marsh, "where you can buy tables and chairs, and pretty artistic cloths, and little whatnots of all descriptions. I'd advise you to go to Rigg's. He's in the High Street, No. 48."

"But Spilman has the most elegant articles, you know, Lucy," interposed Miss Day. "I'll walk over to Spilman's tomorrow with you if you like, Miss Peel."

Before Priscilla had time to reply there again came a knock at the door, and this time Nancy Banister, looking flushed and pretty, walked in.

She took in the scene at a glance.

"How tired you look, Miss Peel!" said Nancy Banister.

Priscilla smiled gratefully at her.

"And your trunk is not unpacked yet?"

"Oh! There is time enough," faltered Priscilla.

"Are we in your way?" spoke Miss Marsh suddenly, springing to her feet. "Good night. My name is Marsh, my room is thirty-eight."

She swung herself lazily and carelessly out of the room, followed, at longer or shorter intervals, by the other girls, who all nodded to Priscilla, told her their names and one or two the numbers of their rooms. At last she was left alone with Nancy Banister.

"Poor thing! How tired and white you look!" said Nancy. "But now that that dreadful martyrdom is over, you shall have a real cozy time. Don't you want a nice, hot cup of cocoa? It will be ready in a minute or two. And please, may I help you to unpack?"

"Thank you," said Priscilla. "If I might have a fire—?" she said suddenly.

"Oh, you poor, shivering darling! Of course. Are there no matches here? There were some on the mantelpiece before dinner. No, I declare they have vanished. How careless of the maid. I'll run into Maggie's room and fetch some."

Miss Banister was not a minute away. She returned with a box of matches, and, stooping down, set a light to the wood. A pleasant fire was soon blazing and crackling merrily.

"Now, isn't that better?" said Nancy. "Please sit down on your bed and give me the key to your trunk. I'll soon have the things out and put all to rights for you. I'm a splendid unpacker."

But Priscilla had no desire to have her small and meager wardrobe overhauled even by the kindest of St. Benet's girls.

"I will unpack presently myself, if you don't mind," she said.

Nancy drew back. "Perhaps you would like me to go away?" she said. "I will go into Maggie's room and let you know when cocoa is ready."

"Thank you," said Prissie. Miss Banister disappeared, and Priscilla sat on by the fire, unconscious that she had given any pain or annoyance, thinking with gratitude of Nancy and Maggie Oliphant, and wondering what her little sisters were doing without her at home tonight.

By and by there came a tap at her door. Priscilla ran to open it. Miss Oliphant stood outside.

"Won't you come in?" said Priscilla, throwing the door wide open and smiling with joy. It was already delightful to her to look at Maggie.

Maggie Oliphant started and turned pale. "Into that room? No, no, I can't," she said in a queer voice. She rushed back to her own, leaving Priscilla standing in amazement by her open door.

There was a moment's silence. Then Miss Oliphant's voice— rich, soft, and lazy—was heard within the shelter of her own apartment.

"Please come in, Miss Peel; cocoa awaits you. Do not stand on ceremony."

Priscilla went timidly across the corridor and instantly found herself in one of the prettiest of the students' rooms at St. Benet's. The room was crowded with knickknacks and rendered gay and sweet by many tall flowers in pots. A piano stood open by one of the walls and a violin lay carelessly on a chair not far off. There were piles of new music and some tempting, small, neatly-bound books lying about. A fire glowed on the hearth and a little brass kettle sang merrily on the hob. The cocoa table was drawn up in front of the fire, and on a quaintly-shaped tray stood the bright little cocoa pot and cups and saucers.

"Welcome to St. Benet's!" said Maggie, going up and taking Priscilla's hand cordially within her own. "Now you'll have to get into this low chair and make yourself quite at home and happy."

"How snug you are here," said Prissie, her eyes brightening and a pink color mounting into her cheeks. She was glad that Maggie was alone; she felt more at ease with her than with anyone.

Maggie poured out a cup of cocoa and brought it to her. Then, drawing another chair forward, she seated herself in it, sipped her own cocoa, and began to talk.

Long afterward Priscilla remembered that talk. It was not what Maggie said, for her conversation in itself was not at all brilliant, but it was the sound of her rich, calm, rather lazy voice, the different lights which glanced and gleamed in her eyes, the dimples about her mouth, the attitude she put herself in. Sometimes the beautiful oval of her face would be almost ivory white, but then a rosy cloud would well up and up the cheeks and ever slightly suffuse the broad, low forehead. Her face was never long the same.

The girls grew cozy and confidential together. Priscilla told Maggie about her home, a little also about her past history and her motive in coming to St. Benet's. Maggie sympathized with all the expression she was capable of. At last Priscilla bade her new friend good night, and, rising from her luxurious chair, prepared to go back to her own room.

She had just reached the door of Maggie's room and was about to turn the handle when a sudden thought arrested her. She came back a few steps.

"May I ask you a question?" she said.

"Certainly," replied Miss Oliphant.

"Who is the girl who used to live in my room? Annabel Lee, the other girls call her. Who is she? What is there remarkable about her?"

To Priscilla's astonishment, Maggie interlocked one soft hand inside the other; her face grew white, hard, and strained.

"You must not ask me about Annabel Lee," she said in a whisper, "for I—I can tell you nothing about her. I can *never* tell you about her. . . ."

Someone touched Priscilla softly on her shoulder.

"Let me take you to your room, Miss Peel," said Nancy Banister.

The two bid good-bye to Maggie, and Nancy took Priscilla's hand and walked with her across the corridor.

"I am so sorry I said anything to hurt Miss Oliphant," said Priscilla.

"Oh, you were not to blame. You could not know any better. Of course, now that you do know, you will never do it again."

"But I don't know anything now. Please will *you* tell me who Annabel Lee is?"

"Annabel Lee"—Nancy's eyes filled with tears—"no girl in the college was so popular."

"Why do you say *was?*"

"Annabel Lee is dead."

"Oh!"

Priscilla walked into her room and Nancy went back to Maggie Oliphant.

§IV§

An Eavesdropper

he students at St. Benet's were accustomed to unlimited license in the matter of sitting up at night. At a certain hour the electric lights were put out, but each girl was well-supplied with candles and could sit up and pursue her studies into the small hours if she willed.

It was late when Priscilla left Maggie Oliphant's room on this first night, but the events of the evening had excited her, and she did not care to go to bed. Her fire was now burning well, and her room was warm and cozy. She drew the bolt of her door, and, unlocking her trunk, began to unpack. Miss Ruby Peel had instilled order into Priscilla from her earliest days, and she now quickly disposed of her small but neat wardrobe. Her linen would just fit into the drawers of the bureau. Her two or three dresses and jackets were hung tidily away behind the curtain that formed her wardrobe.

She undressed with a certain sense of luxuriousness and pleasure. Her room began to look charming to her now that her things were unpacked, and the first sharp pain of her homesickness was greatly softened since she had spent time with Maggie Oliphant.

Priscilla had not often in the course of her life undressed by a fire, but then had she ever spent an evening like this one? All was fresh to her—new and exciting. She got into bed, and, putting out her candle, lay down. The firelight played on the pale blue walls and lit up the bold design of the briar roses which ran round the walls at the top of the room.

She did not believe in ghosts, but she had an uncomfortable sensation, and it would not have greatly surprised her if Annabel had come gliding back in the night watches to put the finishing touches upon the wildflowers that ornamented the panels of the door, and upon the design of the briar rose. Annabel might come in and pursue this work, then glide up to her, ask her to get out of this little white bed, and let her rest in it herself once more.

Annabel Lee! It was a queer name—a wild, bewitching sort of a name—the name of a girl in a song.

Priscilla knew many of Poe's strange songs, and she found herself now murmuring some words which used to fascinate her long ago:

> "But our love it was stronger by far than the love
> Of those who were older than we—
> Of many far wiser than we;
> And neither the angels in heaven above,
> Nor the demons down under the sea,
> Can ever dissever my soul from the soul
> Of the beautiful Annabel Lee."

Some ashes fell from the expiring fire, and Priscilla jumped up in bed with a start. She stretched out her hand for a box of matches. She would light her candle, and, as there was no chance of her going to sleep, sit up, put her dressing-jacket on, and begin to write a long letter home to Aunt Ruby and her little sisters. Such methodical work would calm her.

She rose and, fetching her neat little leather writing case from where she had placed it on the top of her bureau, prepared to open it.

The little case was locked. Priscilla went over to her curtained wardrobe, pushed it aside, and felt for her purse in the pocket of the dress she had worn that day. It was not there. Within that purse the little key was safely hiding, but the purse itself was nowhere to be found.

Priscilla looked all around the room. She stood still for a moment in perplexity. Suppose her purse were gone? Suppose it had been stolen? The very small supply of money which that purse contained was most precious to Priscilla. It seemed to her that nothing could well be more terrible than to ask Aunt Ruby for fresh funds.

Suddenly, as she stood in the middle of her room, a memory came back to her. Something had dropped on the floor as she sat by Maggie's side at dinner. She had felt too nervous and miserable at the time to take any notice of the slight sound made by the fall, but now it returned vividly to her memory. She was sure that her purse must have dropped out of her pocket at that moment, and she was convinced that it was now lying quietly under the table where she had sat.

Priscilla felt far too excited to wait until the morning to make herself sure on this point. Partly re-dressing, she took her candle in her hand, and when she opened the door wide it did not creak. The long corridor outside had a stone floor and was richly carpeted. No fear of treacherous, creaking boards here. Priscilla was prepared to walk briskly down the length of the corridor when she was arrested by seeing a light streaming out of Maggie Oliphant's room.

The electric lights were all extinguished, and this light alone shone like a ray in the darkness.

Prissie stood still with a gasp of dismay. She did not want Maggie to hear her now. She felt sure that a girl like Maggie Oliphant could never understand what a little purse, which only contained a sovereign or two, would mean to her.

On tiptoe, and shading the candle with her hand, she stole past the partly-open door. A rich tapestry curtain hung at the other side, and Maggie doubtless thought the door was shut.

Priscilla had almost gone past the open door when her steps were again arrested by the sound of voices. Someone said "Priscilla Peel," and then someone else laughed.

Priscilla stood perfectly still. Of course she had no right to listen, but she did anyway.

"I would not be jealous if I were you, Nancy," said Maggie's lazy, sweet voice. "The poor girl is as queer as her name, but it gives me a kind of pleasure to be good to people."

Priscilla raised one trembling hand and noiselessly put out her candle. Her feet seemed rooted to the spot.

Nancy murmured something which Priscilla could not hear. Then Maggie's light laugh was heard again.

"The unfortunate girl has fallen for you, there's no doubt about that, Maggie," said Nancy.

"Well, my dear, she'll get over that presently. When I'm kind to them, they all get that grateful, affectionate expression in their eyes. The fact is, Nancy, I have a perfectly crazy desire to make people love me."

"But do you give love, Maggie? Do you give it in return?"

"Sometimes. I don't know. I believe I am rather fond of you, for instance."

"Maggie, was Geoffrey Hammond at St. Hilda's this afternoon?"

"I can't possibly say," replied Maggie in a cold voice. Then she added excitedly, "I don't believe the door is shut! You are so careless, Nancy, so indifferent to the fact that there *may* be eavesdroppers about."

Priscilla crept back to her room. She had forgotten all about her purse. Every other feeling was completely swallowed up in a burning, choking sense of anger.

❧V❧

Priscilla's Past

riscilla had received a shock, and hers was not the sort of nature to take such a blow easily. Priscilla had a rather commonplace past, but it was the sort of past to foster and deepen the peculiarities of her character. Her father had died when she was twelve, her mother when she was fourteen. They were north-country folk, and they were rigidly upright people. They never went into debt; they considered luxuries bad for the soul and the smaller refinements of life altogether unnecessary.

Mr. Peel managed to save a little money out of his earnings. Year by year he took these savings to the nearest county bank and invested them to the best of his ability. The bank broke, and in one fell stroke he lost all the savings of his lifetime. This affected his health, and he never recovered again.

He died and, two years afterward, his wife followed him. Priscilla was then fourteen and there were three little sisters several years younger than her. They were merry little children—strong, healthy, untouched by care. Priscilla, on the contrary, was grave and seemed much older than her years.

On the night their mother was buried, Aunt Ruby, their father's sister, came from her home far away on the borders of Devonshire and told the four desolate children that she was going to take them away to live on her little farm with her.

Aunt Ruby spoke in a very frank manner. "It's only fair to tell you, Prissie," she said, addressing the tall, gawky girl, who stood with her hands folded in front of her, "that how I'm to fill four extra mouths the Lord knows, but I don't. Still, I'm going to try, for it shall never be said that Andrew Peel's children wanted bread while his sister, Ruby Peel, lived."

"We have none of us big appetites," said Priscilla after a long, solemn pause. "We can do with very little food—very little. The only one who ever is *really* hungry is Hattie."

Aunt Ruby looked up at the pale face, for Prissie was taller than her aunt even then, and said in a shocked voice, "Good gracious, child! Do you think I'd stint one of you? You ought all to be hearty, and I hope you will be. No, no, it isn't that, Prissie, but there'll be no luxuries, so don't you expect them."

"I don't want them," answered Priscilla.

The children all went to Devonshire, and Aunt Ruby toiled, as perhaps no woman had ever toiled before, to put bread into their mouths. Nobody thought about the children's education, and they might have grown up without any were it not for Priscilla, who taught them what she knew herself. Nobody thought Priscilla brilliant, but she had a great gift for acquiring knowledge. Wherever she went she picked up a fresh fact, or a fresh fancy, or a new idea, and these she turned over and over in her brain until she made them part of herself.

Among the few things that had been saved from her early home was a box of her father's old books, and these comprised several of the early poets and essayists.

One day the old clergyman who lived at a small vicarage nearby called to see Miss Peel. He discovered Priscilla deep over Carlyle's *History of the French Revolution*. The young girl had become absorbed in the fascination of the wild and terrible tale. Some of the horror of it had got into her eyes as she raised them to return Mr. Hayes' courteous greeting. His attention was arrested by the look she gave him. He questioned her about her reading, and presently offered to help her.

Priscilla made rapid progress. She was not taught in the ordinary fashion, but she was truly being educated. Yet she knew nothing about the world, nothing about society. She had no ambitions and she did not trouble herself to look very far ahead. The old classics which she studied from morning till night abundantly satisfied her strong intellectual nature.

Sometime between her sixteenth and seventeenth birthday, Priscilla was reading in the old parlor of the cottage when the two older children rushed in with the news that Aunt Ruby had suddenly lain flat down in the hayfield, and they thought she was asleep.

Prissie's book tumbled to the floor, she rushed down to the hayfield, and in a moment she was kneeling by Miss Peel's side.

"What is it, Aunt Ruby?" she asked tenderly. "Are you ill?"

The tired woman opened her eyes slowly.

"I think I fainted, dear love," she said. "Perhaps it was the heat of the sun."

Priscilla managed to get her aunt back into the house. She grew better presently and seemed something like herself, but that evening the aunt and niece had a long talk, and the next day Prissie went up to see Mr. Hayes.

"Sit down, Prissie," he said. "I see you are excited. What is the matter?"

"I want you to help me, Mr. Hayes. Will you help me? You have always been my dear friend, my good friend."

"Of course I will help you. What is wrong? Speak to me fully."

"Aunt Ruby fainted in the hay-field yesterday."

"Indeed? Would she like to see me? Is she better today?"

"She is quite well today—quite well for the time."

"I must earn money as soon as it is possible for a girl to do so, and I must stop dreaming and thinking of nothing but books.

"My dear Priscilla, what a tragic face! Your Aunt Ruby is not the first woman who has fainted and been none the worse."

"That is just the point, Mr. Hayes. Aunt Ruby *is* the worse."

Mr. Hayes looked hard into his pupil's face.

He took one of the girl's thin, unformed hands between his own.

"My dear child," he said, "something weighs on your mind. Tell your old friend—your almost father—all that is in your heart."

Thus prompted, Priscilla told the tragic story. Aunt Ruby was affected with an incurable illness. It would not kill her soon; she might live for years, but every year she would grow a little weaker and a little less capable of toil. As long as she lived, the little farm belonged to her, but whenever she died it would pass to a distant cousin. Whenever Aunt Ruby died, Priscilla and her three sisters would be penniless.

"So I have come to you," continued Prissie, "to say that I must take steps at once to enable myself to earn money. I must support Hattie and Rose and Katie whenever Aunt Ruby goes. I must earn money as soon as it is possible for a girl to do so, and I must stop dreaming and thinking of nothing but books, for perhaps books and I will have little to say to each other in the future."

"That would be sad," replied Mr. Hayes, "for that would be taking a directly opposite direction to the path that Providence clearly intends you to walk."

Priscilla raised her eyes and looked earnestly at the old rector.

"How do you propose to earn bread for yourself and your sisters?"

"I thought of dressmaking."

"Um! Did you—make—the gown you have on?"

"Yes," replied Priscilla, looking down at her ungainly home-spun garment.

The rector rose to his feet and smiled.

"I am no judge of such matters," he said, "and I may be wrong. But my impression is that the style and cut of that dress would scarcely have a large demand in fashionable quarters."

"Oh, sir!" Prissie blushed all over. "You know I said I should have to learn."

"My dear child," said Mr. Hayes firmly, "when it becomes a question of a woman earning her bread, let her turn to that path where promise lies. There is no promise in the fit of that gown, Prissie. But here—here there is much."

He touched her forehead lightly with his hand.

"You must not give up your books, my dear," he said, "for, independently of the pleasure they afford, they will also give you bread and butter. Go home now and let me think over matters. Come again tomorrow. I may have important things to say to you."

Mr. Hayes left no stone unturned to effect his object. He thought Priscilla could do brilliantly as a teacher, and he resolved that for this purpose she should have the advantages that only a collegiate life could offer her. He himself prepared her for her entrance examination. Shortly after the completion of her eighteenth year, he and Aunt Ruby between them managed the necessary funds to give the girl a three-years' education as a student at St. Benet's college for women.

Prissie knew very little about the money part of the scheme. She only guessed what had become of Aunt Ruby's watch and chain; and a look of grief crossed her face when one day she happened to see that Aunt Ruby's poor little jewel case was empty. The jewels and the watch could certainly not fetch much, but they provided Prissie with a modest little outfit.

Priscilla bade her sisters, her aunt, and the old rector goodbye and started on her new life with courage.

᚛VI᚜

College Life

The routine of life at St. Benet's was something as follows:

The dressing-bell was rung at seven, and all the students were expected to meet in the chapel for prayers at eight. Nothing was said if they did not appear, but in the three halls known wishes were always regarded, and, as a rule, there were few absentees.

The girls went to chapel in their white-straw sailor hats, simply trimmed with a broad band of ribbon of the college colors, green with a narrow stripe of gold. Breakfast immediately followed chapel; tea and coffee and different cold meats were placed on the side tables, and the girls helped themselves to what they pleased.

The great event at breakfast was the post. Each student, when she entered the breakfast hall, would make an eager rush to the side table where the letters were neatly placed. During breakfast these were read and greatly discussed. The whole meal was most informal and seldom lasted more than a quarter of an hour.

After breakfast the notice board in the large entrance hall was visited and eagerly scanned, for it contained a detailed account of the hours for the different lectures and the names of the lecturers who would instruct the students during the day. By the side of the large official notice board hung another, which was read with quite as deep interest. This contained particulars of the meetings of the different clubs and societies for pleasure or profit which were got up by the girls themselves.

On the morning after her arrival, Priscilla, with the other students, read the contents of these two boards, and then, in the company of a fresher nearly as shy as herself, wandered about the lovely grounds which surrounded Heath Hall until lectures began at nine o'clock.

Lectures continued without interruption until lunchtime, a meal which was taken very much when the girls pleased. The time allowed for this light midday refreshment was from half past twelve to two. The afternoons were mostly given up to games and gymnastics, although occasionally there were more lectures, and the more studious of the girls spent a considerable part of the time studying in their own rooms.

Tea was the sociable meal of the day. To this the girls invited outside friends and acquaintances, and, as a rule, they always took it in their own rooms.

Dinner was at half past six, and from half past seven to half past nine was usually the time when the different clubs and societies met.

There was a regularity and yet a freedom about the life; invisible bounds were prescribed, beyond which no right-minded or conscientious girl cared to venture, but the rules were really very few. Students might visit their friends in Kingsdene and receive them at the college. They might entertain them at luncheon or dinner or at tea in their own rooms, provided the

Teatime

The custom of drinking tea between the luncheon and dinner hours is an almost indispensable part of the domestic routine. The hostess, or whoever presides over the teapot, should see that her chair is one that allows unrestricted freedom of movement, as the pouring of tea possesses possibilities of its own for displaying to advantage the graces of figure and motion.

Taste in the matter of teapots is almost as varied as the designs of the teapots themselves, and the only advice worth offering is to have the daintiest and best you can afford. A "cozy," which is a wadded covering made to fit over the pot to keep it warm while the tea "draws," is another essential.

As to the making of tea, it may not be out of place to say here that it is worthwhile to learn the right way. English visitors to America sometimes complain that the Americans make poor tea. Many of them do, undoubtedly. There are even benighted souls here and there who believe in boiled tea, or who would look at one in mild surprise if told that the beverage which has been steeping in the teapot on the back of the stove during the whole afternoon is not quite as good as the fresh-made cup.

—The Modern Hostess, 1904

friends left at a certain hour. And if the girls themselves asked for leave of absence when they wished to remain out and mentioned the place to which they proposed to go, no objections were offered.

They were expected to return to the college not later than eleven at night, and one invitation to go out in the week was, as a rule, the most they ever accepted.

Into this life Priscilla came, fresh from the Devonshire farm. After a few days, however, she fitted into her new grooves, took up the line of study which she intended to pursue, and was quickly absorbed in all the fascinations it offered to a nature like hers.

Her purse was restored to her on the morning after her arrival, and neither Maggie Oliphant nor Nancy Banister ever guessed that she had overheard some words of theirs and that these had put bitterness into her heart. Both Maggie and Nancy made several overtures of kindness to Prissie, but the cold manner that was more or less habitual to her never thawed, and, after a time, they left her alone. There is no saying what might have happened to Prissie had she never overheard this conversation. As it was, however, after the first shock it gave her courage.

She said to herself: "I should think very little of myself if I did not despise a girl like Miss Oliphant. Is it likely I should care to imitate one whom I despise? There was a brief, dreadful hour when I absolutely pined to have pretty things in my room as she has in hers; now I can do without them. My room shall remain bare and unadorned. In this state it will at least look unique."

It did. The other students who lived in the same corridor came to visit Priscilla in the free and easy manner which characterized them and made remarks the reverse of flattering. When *was* she going to put her pictures up? Miss Day would be delighted to help her whenever she chose to do it. When did she intend to go down to Kingsdene to order her easy chairs and little Japanese tables and rugs and the other small but necessary articles that would be required to make her room habitable?

For several days Priscilla turned these inquiries aside. She blushed, stammered, looked awkward, and spoke of something else. At last, however, she summoned up courage, and once and for all delivered herself from her tormentors.

It was evening and Miss Day, Miss Marsh, and Nancy Banister had all come in for a few minutes to see Priscilla on their way to their own rooms.

"Do come and cocoa with me tonight, Miss Peel," said Miss Day. "You're so dreadfully unsociable, not a bit like an ordinary St. Benet's girl."

"I am accustomed to a very quiet life," responded Priscilla, "and I want to work; I have come here to work."

"Oh, nonsense!" said Miss Marsh. "St. Benet's was made for sociability as well as study, and I have no patience with the students who don't try to combine the two. By the way," she added, "I sent you a message to say I was going down to Kingsdene this afternoon and would be happy to take you with me if you would care to visit Spilman's."

"Thank you," said Priscilla, "I got your note just too late to answer it. I was going to speak to you about it," she added.

"Then you would have come?"

Priscilla's face grew very red.

"No, I should not have come."

It was Miss Marsh's turn to get red.

"Come! Annie," she exclaimed, turning to Miss Day, "we had better waste no more time here. Miss Banister, we'll see you presently, won't we? Good night, Miss Peel. Perhaps you don't mind my saying something very frank?"

"I do," said Priscilla, "but that won't prevent your saying it, will it?"

"I don't think it will. After you have been at St. Benet's a little longer you will know that we not only appreciate cleverness and studious ways, but also obliging and sociable and friendly manners; and—and—pretty rooms—rooms with easy chairs and comfortable lounges and the thousand-and-one things which give one a feeling of home. Take my advice, Miss Peel, there's no use fighting against the tide. You'll have to do as others do in the long run, and you may as well do it at once. That is my plain opinion, and I should not have given it to you if I had not thought you needed it. Good night."

"Take my advice, Miss Peel, there's no use fighting against the tide. You'll have to do as others do in the long run, and you may as well do it at once."

"No, stop a minute," said Priscilla. Every scrap of color had left her face. She walked before the two girls to the door and closed it. "Please stay just for a minute longer, Miss Day and Miss Marsh, and you too, Miss Banister, if you will."

She went across the room again, and, opening the top drawer of her bureau, took out her purse. Out of the purse she took a key. The key fitted a small padlock and the padlock belonged to her trunk. She unlocked her empty trunk and opened it.

"There," she said, turning to the girls, "you will be good enough to notice that there are no photographs concealed in this trunk, no pictures, no prints." She lifted the tray. "Empty, you see," she added, pointing with her hand to the lower portion of the trunk—"nothing here to make my room pretty and cozy and homelike." Then she shut the trunk again and locked it, and going up to where the three girls stood gazing at her in bewilderment and some alarm, she unfastened her purse and turned all its contents into the palm of her hand.

"Look, Miss Marsh," she said, turning to the girl who had spoken last. "You may count what is here. One sovereign, one half-sovereign, two or three shillings, some pence. Would this money go far at Spilman's, do you think?"

Priscilla put it all slowly back again into her purse. Her face was still absolutely colorless. She laid the purse on the top of her bureau.

"I do not suppose," she said in a low, sad voice, "that I am the sort of girl who often comes to a place of this sort. I am poor, and I have got to work hard, and I have no time for pleasure. Nevertheless," she added—and now a great wave of color swept over her face, and her eyes were lit up, and she had a sensation of feeling quite glad, and strong, and happy—"I am not going away because I am poor, and I am not going to mind what anyone thinks of me as long as I do right. My room must stay empty and bare, because I have no money to make it full and beautiful. And do you think that I would ask those—those who sent me here—to add one feather's weight to their cares and expenses, to give me money to buy beautiful things because I am afraid of you? No, I should be *awfully* afraid to do that; but I am not afraid of you."

Priscilla opened the drawer of her bureau and put her little, light purse back again in its hiding place.

"Good night, Miss Peel," said Miss Day in a thin, small kind of voice.

"Good night, Miss Peel," said Miss Marsh. The girls went gently out of the room. They closed the door behind them without making any noise. Nancy Banister remained behind. She came up to Priscilla and kissed her.

"You are brave," she said. "I admire you. I—I— am proud of you. I am glad to know that a girl like you has come to live here."

"Don't—don't," said poor Prissie. Her little burst of courage had deserted her. She covered her face with her trembling hands. She did not want Nancy Banister to see that her eyes were full of tears.

৶VII৶

In Miss Oliphant's Room

y dear," said Nancy Banister that same evening—"my dear and beloved Maggie, we have both been guilty of a huge mistake."

"What is that?" asked Miss Oliphant. She was leaning back in a deep easy chair, and Nancy had perched herself on a little stool at her feet. Nancy was a small, nervous-looking person; she had a zealous face and eager, almost too-active movements. Nancy was the soul of bustling good nature, of brightness and kindness. She often said that Maggie Oliphant's laziness rested her.

"What is it?" said Maggie again. "How are we in the wrong, Nancy?"

She lifted her dimpled hand as she spoke and contemplated it with a slow, satisfied sort of smile.

"We have made a mistake about Miss Peel, that is all; she is a very noble girl."

"Oh, my dear Nance! Poor little Puritan Prissie! What next?"

"It is all very fine to call her names," replied Nancy—here she sprang to her feet—"but *I* couldn't do what she did. Do you know that she absolutely and completely turned the tables on that vulgar Annie Day and that pushing, silly little Lucy Marsh? I never saw any two look smaller or poorer than those two when they skedaddled out of her room. Yes, that's the word—they skedaddled to the door, both of them, looking as limp as a cotton dress when it has been worn for a week, and one almost treading on the other's heels; and I do not think Prissie will be worried by them anymore."

"Really, Nancy, you look quite pretty when you are excited! Now, what did this wonderful Miss Peel do? Did she box the ears of those two detestable girls? If so, she has my hearty congratulations."

"More than that, Maggie—that poor, little, meek, awkward, slim creature absolutely demolished them. Oh! She did it in such a fine, simple sort of way. I only wish you had seen her! They were twitting her about not going in for all the fun here and, above everything, for keeping her room so bare and unattractive. You know there isn't a room in the hall like hers—it's so bare and unhomelike. What's the matter, Maggie?"

"You needn't go on, Nancy; if it's about the room, I don't want to hear it. You know I can't—I can't bear it."

Maggie's lips were trembling, her face was white.

"Oh, my darling, I am so sorry. I forgot—I really did! There, you must try and think it was any room. What she did was all the same. She opened her little trunk. I really could have cried. It was such a poor, pathetic sort of receptacle to be capable of holding all one's worldly goods, and she showed it to them—empty! 'You see,' she said, 'that I have no pictures nor ornaments here!' Then she turned the contents of her purse into her hand. I think, Maggie, she had about thirty shillings in the world, and she asked Lucy Marsh to count her money, and inquired how many things she thought it would purchase at Spilman's. Her eyes had such a splendid, good, brave sort of light in them. And she said she had come here to work, and she meant to work, and her room must stay bare, for she had no money to make it anything else. 'But,' she said, 'I am not afraid of you, but I *am* afraid of hurting those'—whoever 'those' are—'who have sent me here!'

"Oh, Maggie, I wish you wouldn't talk in that reckless way nor pretend that you hate goodness. You know you adore it—you know you do!"

"After that the two girls skedaddled; they had had enough of her, and I expect, Maggie, your little Puritan Prissie will be left in peace in the future."

"Don't call her my little Puritan," said Maggie. "I have nothing to say to her."

Maggie was leaning back again in her chair now; her face was still pale and her soft eyes looked troubled.

"I wish you wouldn't tell me heroic stories, Nancy," she remarked after a pause. "They make me feel so uncomfortable. If Priscilla Peel is going to be turned into a sort of heroine, she'll be much more unbearable than in her former character."

"Oh, Maggie, I wish you wouldn't talk in that reckless way nor pretend that you hate goodness. You know you adore it— you know you do! You know you are far and away the most lovable and good—the very best girl at St. Benet's."

"No, dear little Nancy, you are quite mistaken. I'm *not* lovable and I'm *not* good. There, my dear, do let us turn from that uninteresting person—Maggie Oliphant. And so, Nancy, you are going to worship Priscilla Peel in future?"

"Oh, dear no! That's not my way. But I'm going to respect her very much. I think we have both rather shunned her lately, and I *did* feel sure at first that you meant to be very kind to her, Maggie."

Maggie yawned. It was her way to get over emotion very quickly. A moment before her face had been all eloquent with feeling; now its expression was distinctly bored, and her lazy eyes were not even open to their full extent.

"Perhaps I would have continued to be kind if she had reciprocated attentions, but she did not. Are you going, Nancy?"

"Yes, I promised to have cocoa with Annie Day. I had almost forgotten. Good night, Maggie."

Nancy shut the door softly behind her, and Maggie closed her eyes for a moment with a sigh of relief.

Maggie curled herself up in her luxurious chair, arranged a soft pillow under her head, and shut her eyes. This lasted for a short time, perhaps ten minutes. Then the falling of a coal in the grate disturbed the slumber of the sleeper. Maggie stirred restlessly and turned her head. She was dreaming. Presently tears stole from under the black eyelashes and rolled down her cheeks. She opened her eyes wide; she was awake again; unutterable regret, remorse, which might never be quieted, filled her face.

Maggie rose from her chair and, going across the room, sat down at the bureau. She turned a shaded lamp so that the light might fall upon the pages of a book she was studying and, pushing her hands through her thick hair, she began to read a passage from the splendid *Prometheus Vinctus* of Aeschylus:

"O divine ether, O swift-winged winds!"

She muttered the opening lines to herself, then turning the page continued to translate from the Greek with great ease and fluency.

Anyone who had seen Maggie in her deep and expressionless sleep but a few minutes before would have watched her now with a sensation of surprise. This queer girl was showing yet another phase of her complex nature. Her face was no longer stricken with sorrow. Now, intellect and the triumphant delight of overcoming a mental difficulty reigned supreme in her face. She read on without interruption for nearly an hour. At the end of that time her cheeks were burning like two glowing crimson roses.

A knock came at her door.

"It's just my luck," muttered Maggie. "I'd have got the sense of that whole magnificent passage in another hour. I'd have had a good night if that knock hadn't come—but now—now I am Maggie Oliphant, the most miserable girl at St. Benet's, once again."

The knock was repeated. Maggie sprang to her feet.

"Come in," she said.

The handle of the door was slowly turned, the tapestry curtain moved forward, and a little fair-haired girl, with an infantile expression of face and looking years younger than her eighteen summers, tripped a few steps into the room.

"I beg your pardon, Maggie," she said. "I had not a moment to come sooner—not one really. That stupid Miss Turner chose to raise the alarm for the fire brigade. Of course I had to go, and I've only just come back and changed my dress."

"You ought to be in bed, Rosalind; it's past eleven o'clock."

"Oh, as if that mattered! I'll go in a minute. How cozy you look here."

"My dear, I am not going to keep you out of your beauty sleep. You can admire my room another time. If you have a message for me, Rosalind, let me have it."

Rosalind Merton had serene, baby-blue eyes; they looked up now full at Maggie. Then her dimpled little hand slid swiftly into the pocket of her dress and came out again with a square envelope with some manly writing on it.

"There," said Rosalind, "that's for you. I was at Kingsdene to-day—and—I—said you should have it, and I—I promised that I'd *help* you, Maggie. I said I would help you, if you'd let me."

"Thank you," replied Maggie in a lofty tone. The words came out of her lips with the coldness of ice. "And if I need you, I promise to ask your help. Where did you say you met Mr. Hammond?"

Maggie took up her letter and opened it slowly.

"At Spilman's. He was buying something for his room. He—" Rosalind blushed all over her face.

Maggie took her letter out of its envelope. She looked at the first two or three words, then laid it, open as it was, on the table.

"Thank you, Rosalind," she said in her usual tone. "It was kind of you to bring this, certainly. But Mr. Hammond would have done better had he sent his letter by post. There would have been no mystery about it then, and I should have received it at least two hours ago. Thank you, Rosalind, all the same—good night."

Rosalind Merton stepped demurely out of the room. In the corridor, however, a change come over her small, childish face. Her blue eyes became full of angry flame and she clenched her hand and shook it in the direction of the closed door.

"Oh, Maggie Oliphant, what a deceiver you are!" she murmured. "You think that I'm a baby and notice nothing, but I'm on the alert now, and I'll watch—and watch. I don't love you any longer, Maggie Oliphant. Who loves being snubbed? Oh, of course, you pretend you don't care about that letter! But I know you *do* care; and I'll get hold of all your secrets before many weeks are over, see if I don't!"

59

❧VIII❧

The Most Comforting Way

 aggie was once more alone. She ran to the door and drew the bolt; then, sinking down once more in her easy chair, she took up the letter that Rosalind Merton had brought her and began to read its contents. Both sides of a sheet of paper were covered with small, close writing, the neat, somewhat cramped hand which at that time characterized the men of St. Hilda's College.

Maggie's eyes seemed to fly over the writing; they absorbed the sense, they took the full meaning from each word. At last all was known to her, burnt in, indeed, upon her brain.

She crushed the letter suddenly in one of her hands, then raised it to her lips and kissed it; then fiercely, as though she hated it, tossed it into the fire. After this she sat quiet, her hands folded meekly, her head slightly bent. The color gradually left her cheeks. After a time she rose, and, walking very slowly across her room, sat down by her bureau and drew a sheet of paper before her. As she did so her eyes fell for a moment on the Greek play which had fascinated her an hour ago. She found herself again murmuring some lines from *Prometheus Vinctus*:

"O divine ether, and swift-winged winds—"

"Folly!" she murmured, pushing the book aside. "Even glorious, great thoughts like those don't satisfy me. Whoever supposed they would? What was I given a heart for? Why does it beat so fiercely, and long, and love? And why is it wrong—wrong of me to love? Oh, Annabel Lee! Oh, darling! If only your wretched Maggie Oliphant had never known you!"

Maggie dashed some heavy tears from her eyes. Then, taking up her pen, she began to write.

> "HEATH HALL,
>
> "ST. BENET'S.
>
> "DEAR MR. HAMMOND: I should prefer that you did not in future give letters for me to any of my friends here. Please understand this. When you have anything to say to me, you can write in the ordinary course of post. I am not ashamed of any slight correspondence we may have together; but I refuse to countenance, or to be in any sense a party to, what may even seem underhand.
>
> "I shall try to be at the Marshalls' on Sunday afternoon, but I have nothing to say in reply to your letter. My views are unalterable.
>
> "Yours sincerely,
>
> "MARGARET OLIPHANT."

Maggie did not read the letter after she had written it. She put it into an envelope and directed it:

> GEOFFREY HAMMOND, ESQ.,
> St. Hilda's,
> Kingsdene.

She stamped her letter and, late as it was, took it down herself and deposited it in the post-bag.

The next morning when the students strolled in to breakfast, many pairs of eyes were raised with a new curiosity to watch Priscilla Peel. Even Maggie, as she drank her coffee and munched a piece of dry toast—for she was a very poor eater—could not help flashing a keen and interested glance at the young girl as she came into the room.

"The conceit of some people! Of all forms of conceit, preserve me from the priggish style."

Prissie was the reverse of fashionable in her attire; her neat brown cashmere dress had been made by Aunt Ruby. The hemming, the stitching, the gathering, the frilling that went to make up this useful garment were neat; but Aunt Ruby was not gifted with a stylish cut. Prissie's hair was smoothly parted, but the thick plait on the back of the neck was by no means artistically coiled.

The curious girls laughed and turned their heads away. They had heard of her exploit of the night before. Miss Day and Miss Marsh had repeated this good story. It had impressed them at the time, but they did not tell it to others in a positive way. And the girls who heard the tale spoke of her to one another as an "insufferable little prig."

"Isn't it too absurd," said Rosalind Merton, sidling up to Maggie and casting some disdainful glances at poor Priscilla, "the conceit of some people! Of all forms of conceit, preserve me from the priggish style."

"I don't understand you," said Maggie, raising her eyes and speaking in her lazy voice. "Are there any prigs about? I don't see them. Oh, Miss Peel"—she jumped up hastily—"won't you sit here by me? I have been reserving this place for you, for I have been so anxious to know if you would do me a kindness. Please sit down, and I'll tell you what it is. You needn't wait, Rosalind. What I have got to say is for Miss Peel's ears."

Rosalind retired to the other end of the room, and, if the laughing and muttering continued, they now only reached Maggie and Priscilla in the form of very distant murmurs.

"How pale you look," said Maggie, turning to the girl, "and how cold you are! Yes, I am quite sure you are bitterly cold. Now you shall have a good breakfast. Let me help you. Please do. I'll go to the side table and bring you something so tempting; wait and see."

"You mustn't trouble really," began Priscilla.

Miss Oliphant flashed a brilliant smile at her. Priscilla, in spite of herself, felt her coldness begin to thaw. Maggie ran over to the side table and Priscilla kept repeating under her breath:

"She's not true—she's beautiful, but she's false; she has the kindest, sweetest, most comforting way in the world, but she only does it for the sake of selfish pleasure. I ought not to let her. I ought not to speak to her. I ought to go away and have nothing to do with her proffers of goodwill, and yet somehow or other I can't resist her."

Maggie came back with some delicately carved chicken and ham and a hot cup of delicious coffee.

"Is not this nice?" she said. "Now eat it all up and speak to me afterward."

"Do you mean it?" she said in a choked kind of voice.

"Of course! What do you take me for? Why should not I sympathize with you?"

"I want you to," said Prissie. Tears filled her eyes; she turned her head away. Maggie gave her hand a squeeze.

"Now eat your breakfast," she said. "I shall glance through my letters while you are busy."

Rosalind's hat was extremely pretty and becoming, and Priscilla
fancied she got a glimpse of a gay silk dress under her fur-lined coat.

It was one of Miss Oliphant's peculiarities to inspire in others absolute and almost unreasoning faith in herself. Doubts would and might return in her absence, but in the sunshine of her particularly genial manner they found it hard to live.

After breakfast the girls were leaving the room together when Miss Heath, the vice-principal of the hall in which they resided, came into the room. She was a tall, stately woman of about thirty-five and had seen very little of Priscilla since her arrival, but now she stopped to give both girls a special greeting.

"My dear," she said to Prissie, "I have been anxious to cultivate your acquaintance. Will you come and have tea with me in my room this afternoon? And Maggie dear, will you come with Miss Peel?"

She laid her hand on Maggie's shoulder as she spoke, looked swiftly into the young girl's face, then turned with a glance of great interest to Priscilla.

"You will both come," she said. "That is right. I won't ask anyone else. We shall have a cozy time together, and Miss Peel can tell me all about her studies, aims, and ambitions."

"Thank you," said Maggie, "I'll answer for Miss Peel. We shall be delighted."

Miss Heath nodded to the pair and walked swiftly away.

"Is she not charming?" whispered Maggie. "Did I not tell you you would fall in love with Dorothea?"

"But I have not," said Priscilla, coloring.

Maggie checked a petulant exclamation that was rising to her lips. She was conscious of a curious desire to win her queer young companion's goodwill and sympathy.

"Never mind," she said, "the moment of victory is only delayed. You will tell a very different story after you have had tea with Dorothea this evening. Now, let us come and look at the notice boards and see what the day's program is. By the way, are you going to attend any lectures this morning?"

"Yes, two," said Prissie. "One on Middle History, from eleven to twelve, and I have a French lecture afterward."

"Well, I am not doing anything this morning. I wish you were not. We might have taken a long walk together. Don't you love long walks?"

"Oh yes. But there is no time for anything of that sort here . . . nor . . . " Priscilla hesitated. "I don't think there's space for a very long walk here," she added. The color rushed into her cheeks as she spoke and her eyes looked wistful.

Maggie laughed.

"What *are* your ideas in regard to space, Miss Peel? The whole of Kingsdeneshire lies before us. We can go where we please. Is not that a sufficiently broad area for our roamings?"

"But there is no sea," said Priscilla. "We should never have time to walk from here to the sea, and nothing—nothing else seems worthwhile."

"Oh, you have lived by the sea?"

"Yes, all my life. When I was a little girl, my home was near Whitby, in Yorkshire, and lately I have lived close to Lyme— two extreme points of England, you will say; but no matter, the sea is the same. To walk for miles on the top of the cliffs, that means exercise."

"Ah," said Maggie with a sigh, "I understand you—I know what you mean."

She spoke quickly, as she always did under the least touch of excitement. "Such a walk means more than exercise; it means thought, aspiration. Your brain seems to expand then and ideas come. Of course you don't care for poor flat Kingsdeneshire."

Priscilla turned and stared at Miss Oliphant. Maggie laughed. "I must not talk any more," she said, turning pale and shrinking into herself. "Forgive my rhapsodies. You'll understand what they are worth when you know me better. Oh, by the way, will you come with me to Kingsdene on Sunday? We can go to the three o'clock service at the chapel and afterward have tea with some friends of mine—the Marshalls—they'd be delighted to see you."

"What chapel is the service at?" inquired Priscilla.

"What chapel? Is there a second? Come with me and you will never ask that question again. Get under the shade of St. Hilda's—see once those fretted roofs and those painted windows. Listen but once to that angel choir, and then dare to ask me what chapel I mean when I invite you to come and taste of heaven beforehand."

"Thank you," said Priscilla, "I'll come. I cannot be expected to know about things before I have heard of them, can I? But I am very much obliged to you, and I shall be delighted to come."

℘IX℘

A New Life

he vice-principal's room at Heath Hall was double the size of those occupied by the students. In summer, Miss Heath's room was beautiful, for the two deep bay windows—one facing west, the other south—looked out upon smoothly-kept lawns and flower beds, upon tall elm trees, and also upon a distant peep of the river for which Kingsdene was famous. In winter, too, however—and winter had almost come now—the vice-principal's room had a unique effect, and Priscilla never forgot the first time she saw it. The young girl stepped across the threshold of a new life on this evening. She would always remember it.

It was getting dark, and curtains were drawn round the cozy bays and the firelight blazed cheerfully.

There was no one in the room to greet her when she entered. She felt so overmastered by shyness, however, that this was almost a relief, and she sank down into one of the many comfortable chairs with a feeling of thankfulness and looked around her.

The next moment a servant entered with a lamp covered with a gold silk shade. She placed it on a table near the fire and lit a few candles, which stood on carved brackets round the walls. Then Prissie saw what made her forget Miss Heath and her shyness and all else—a great bank of flowers, which stretched across one complete angle of the room. There were some roses, some chrysanthemums, some geraniums. They were cunningly arranged in pots but had the effect of a gay, tropical garden. Prissie rushed to them, knelt down by a tall, white Japanese chrysanthemum, and buried her face in its long, wavy petals.

Prissie had never seen such flowers, and she loved all flowers. Her heart swelled with a kind of wonder.

"My dear child," said Miss Heath behind her, "I am so sorry I was not in the room when you came in; but never mind, my flowers gave you welcome."

"Yes," said Prissie, standing up pale and with a luminous light in her eyes.

"You love flowers?" said Miss Heath, giving her a keen glance.

"Oh yes; but I did not know—I could not guess—that any flower could be as beautiful as this," and she touched the great white chrysanthemum with her finger.

"Yes, and there are some flowers even more wonderful. Have you ever seen orchids?"

"No."

"Then you have something to live for. Orchids are ordinary flowers spiritualized. They have a glamor over them. We have good orchid shows sometimes at Kingsdene. I will take you to the next."

The servant brought in tea, and Miss Heath placed Prissie in a comfortable chair where she was neither oppressed by lamp-light nor firelight.

"A shy little soul like this will love the shade," she said to herself. "For all her plainness this is no ordinary girl, and I mean to draw her out presently. What a brow she has, and what a light came into her eyes when she looked at my white chrysanthemum."

There came a tap at the door and Maggie Oliphant entered, looking fresh and bright. She gave Prissie an affectionate glance and nod and then began to busy herself, helping Miss Heath with the tea. During the meal a little pleasant murmur of conversation was kept up. Miss Heath and Maggie exchanged ideas. They even entered upon one or two delicate little skirmishes, each cleverly arguing a slight point on which they appeared to differ.

They talked of one or two books which were then under discussion; they said a little about music and a word or two with regard to the pictures which were just then causing talk among the art critics in London. It was all new to Prissie, this "light, airy, nothing" kind of talk. Prissie was accustomed to classify everything, but she did not know under what head to put this pleasant conversation. She listened without losing a word. She forgot herself absolutely.

Miss Heath, however, who knew Maggie Oliphant, but did not know Prissie, was observant of the silent young stranger through all the delights of her pleasant talk. Almost imperceptibly she got Prissie to say a word or two. She paused when she saw a question in Prissie's eyes, and her timid and gentle words were listened to with deference. By slow degrees Maggie was the silent one and Priscilla and Miss Heath held the field between them.

"No, I have never been properly educated," Prissie was saying. "I have never gone to a high school. I don't do things in the regular fashion. I was so afraid I should not be able to pass the entrance examination for St. Benet's. I was delighted when I found that I had done so."

"You passed the examination creditably," said Miss Heath. "I have looked through your papers. Your answers were thoughtful. Whoever has educated you, you have been well taught. You can think."

"Oh yes, my dear friend, Mr. Hayes, always said that was the first thing."

"Ah, that accounts for it," replied Miss Heath. "You have had the advantage of listening to a cultivated man's conversation. You ought to do very well here. What do you mean to take up?"

"Oh, everything. I can't know too much."

Miss Heath laughed and looked at Maggie. Maggie was lying back in her easy chair, her head resting luxuriously against a dark velvet cushion. She was tapping the floor slightly with her small foot; her eyes were fixed on Prissie. When Miss Heath laughed Maggie echoed the sound, but both laughs were in the sweetest sympathy.

"You must not overwork yourself, my dear," said Miss Heath. "That would be a very false beginning. I think—I am sure—that you have an earnest and ardent nature, but you must avoid an extreme which will only end in disaster."

Prissie frowned.

"What do you mean?" she said. "I have come here to study. It has been done with such, such difficulty. It would be cruel to waste a moment. I mustn't. You can't mean what you say."

Miss Heath was silent. After a moment she said quietly, "Many girls come to St. Benet's, Miss Peel, who are, I fancy, circumstanced like you. Their friends find it difficult to send them here, but they make the sacrifice, sometimes in one way, sometimes in another—and the girls come. They know it is their duty to study; they know by and by they must pay back."

"Oh, yes," said Priscilla, starting forward and a flush coming into her face. "I know that is what it is for. To pay back worthily—to

71

give back a thousandfold what you have received. Those girls can't be idle, can they?" she added.

"My dear, there have been several such girls at St. Benet's, and none of them has been idle; they have been best and first among our students. Many of them have done more than well—many of them have brought fame to St. Benet's. They are in the world now and earning honorable livelihoods as teachers or in other departments where cultivated women can alone take the field. These girls are all paying back a thousandfold those who have helped them."

"The successful girl here is the girl who takes advantage of the whole life mapped out for her, who divides her time between play and work."

"Yes," said Prissie.

"You would like to follow their example?"

"Oh, yes; please tell me about them."

"Some of them were like you and thought they would take up everything—everything, I mean, in the scholastic line. They filled their days with lectures and studied into the short hours of the night. Maggie, dear, please tell Miss Peel about Good-night and Good-morning."

"They were such a funny pair," said Maggie. "They had rooms next to each other in our corridor, Miss Peel. They were both studying for an honors examination, and during the term before the examination one went to bed at four and one got up at four. Mary Joliffe used to go into Susan Martin's room and say good morning to her. Susan used to raise such a white face and say, 'Good night, my dear.' Well, poor things, neither of them got honors; they worked too hard."

"The simple English of all this," said Miss Heath, "is that the successful girl here is the girl who takes advantage of the whole life mapped out for her, who divides her time between play and work, who joins the clubs and enters heartily into the social life of the place. Yes," she added, looking suddenly full at Priscilla, "these last words of mine may seem strange to you, dear. Believe me, however, they are true."

Priscilla looked unconvinced.

"I must do what you wish," she said, "for, of course, you ought to know."

"What a lame kind of assent, my love! Maggie, you will have to gently lure this young person into the paths of frivolity. I promise you, my dear, that you shall be a very cultivated woman someday; but I only promise this if you will take advantage of all sides of the pleasant life here. Now tell me, what are your particular tastes? What branch of study do you like best?"

"I love Latin and Greek better than anything else in the world."

"Do you truly?" said Maggie, suddenly starting forward. "Then in one thing we have a great sympathy. What have you read? Do tell me."

Miss Heath stepped directly into the background. The two girls conversed for a long time together.

§X§

Mr. Hammond

ere we are now," said Maggie Oliphant, touching her young companion. "This is the outer chapel."

"Yes," answered Priscilla. She spoke in an awed kind of voice.

The cool effect of the dark oak, combined with the richness of the many shafts of colored light coming from the magnificent windows, gave her face a curious expression. Was it caused by emotion or by the strange lights in the chapel?

Maggie glanced at her, touched her hand for a moment, and then hurried forward to her seat.

The girls were accommodated with seats just above the choir. They could read out of the college prayer books and had a fine view of the church.

The congregation streamed in, the choir followed, the curtains were dropped, and the service began. There was no better musical service in England than that which Sunday after Sunday was conducted at St. Hilda's Chapel at Kingsdene. The boys sent up notes as clear and sweet as nightingales into the fretted arches of the roof; the men's deeper notes swelled the

Behavior in Church

No one in a house of worship should do anything to impose the mundane and everyday upon the sanctity of a church. This includes restlessness, whispering, gossiping, paying attention to the dress or actions of others; the vulgar rudeness of sleeping. Whenever possible, sneezing, coughing, and any noise likely to disturb others is to be prohibited.

When a collection is taken up, money should be put into the plate quietly; there should be no ring of coins falling into the platter.

In entering a church in which you are a stranger, either seat yourself quietly in a rear pew or wait for an usher to assign you a place in a pew farther front.

On no account stalk into any open pew which takes your fancy!

Dress in church, while conforming to the time and hour, should be simple. A display of jewels on the part of a woman is particularly out of place.

—The Book of Good Manners, 1923

music until it broke on the ears in a full tide of perfect harmony; the great organ filled in the breaks and pauses. This splendid service of song seemed to reach perfection.

Maggie Oliphant did not come very often to St. Hilda's. At one time she was a constant worshiper there, but that was a year ago, before something happened that changed her. Then, Sunday after Sunday, two lovely girls used to walk up the aisle side by side. The usher knew them and reserved their favorite stall for them. They used to kneel together and listen to the service and, what is more, take part in it.

"During the prayers Maggie wept, but when a great wave of song filled the vast building, she forgot all her sorrow."

But a time came when one of the girls could never return to St. Hilda's and the other, people said, did not care to sit in the old seat without her. They said she missed her friend and was more crushed than anyone else at the sudden death of one so fair and lovely.

When Maggie took her place in the old stall today, more than one person turned to look at her with interest.

Maggie always made a picturesque effect; she wore a large hat, with a drooping plume of feathers; her dress was very rich and dark; her fair face shone in the midst of these surroundings like an exquisite flower.

The service went on. During the prayers Maggie wept, but when a great wave of song filled the vast building, she forgot all her sorrow; her voice rose with the other singers, clear, sweet, and high. Her soul seemed to go up on her voice, for all the sadness left her face; her eyes looked jubilant.

Prissie had never been in any place like St. Hilda's before. It had been one of her dreams to go to the cathedral at Exeter, but year after year this desire of hers had been put off and put off, and this was the first time in her life that she had ever listened to cathedral music. She was impressed, delighted.

"The organ is magnificent," she said to herself, "but not grander than the sea. The sea accompanies all the service at the dear little old church at home."

People met and talked to one another outside the chapel. Several other St. Benet girls had come to the afternoon service. Among them was Miss Day and that fair, innocent-looking little girl, Rosalind Merton.

Miss Day and Miss Merton were together. They were both stepping back to join Maggie and Prissie when a tall, dark young man came hastily forward, bowed to Rosalind Merton, and, coming up to Maggie Oliphant, shook hands with her.

"I saw you in chapel," he said. "Are you coming to the Marshalls' to tea?"

"I am. Let me introduce to you my friend, Miss Peel. Miss Peel, this is Mr. Hammond."

Hammond raised his hat to Prissie, said a courteous word to her, and then turned to speak again to Maggie.

The three walked through the gates and turned up the narrow, picturesque High Street. It would soon be dusk; a wintry light was over everything. Rosalind Merton and Annie Day followed behind. Maggie, who was always absorbed with the present interest, did not heed or notice them, but Priscilla heard one or two ill-bred giggles.

She turned her head with indignation and received scornful glances from both girls. The five met for a moment at a certain corner. Maggie said something to Annie Day and introduced Mr. Hammond to her. As she did so, Rosalind took the opportunity to come up to Priscilla and whisper to her, "You're not wanted, you know. You had much better come home with us."

"What do you mean?" replied Prissie in her matter-of-fact voice. "Miss Oliphant has asked me to go with her to the Marshalls'."

"Oh, well—if you care to be in the—" resumed Rosalind.

Maggie suddenly flashed round on her.

"Come, Miss Peel, we'll be late," she said. "Good-bye." She nodded to Rosalind; her eyes were full of an angry fire. She took Prissie's hand and hurried down the street.

The two girls walked away, still giggling. Maggie turned and began to talk again to Mr. Hammond. Her tone was flippant; her silvery laughter floated in the air. Priscilla turned and gazed at her friend. She was seeing Maggie in yet another aspect. She felt bewildered.

The three presently reached a pleasant house standing on its own grounds. They were shown into a large drawing room, which was full of young people. Mrs. Marshall, a pretty old lady with white hair, came forward to receive them. Maggie was swept away amid fervent embraces and handshakes to the other end of the room. Mrs. Marshall saw that Priscilla looked frightened; she took her under her wing, sat down by her on a sofa, and began to talk.

Prissie answered in a sedate voice. Mrs. Marshall had a very gentle manner. Prissie began to lose her shyness; she almost imagined that she was back with Aunt Ruby again.

"My dear, you will like us all very much," the old lady said. "No life can be so absolutely delightful as that of a girl graduate of St. Benet's. The freedom from care, the mixture of study with play, the pleasant social life—all combine to make young women both healthy and wise.

"Helen," she called to her granddaughter who was standing near, "bring Miss Peel another cup of tea—and some cake, Helen—some of that nice cake you made yesterday. Now, my love, I insist. You don't look at all strong. You really must eat plenty."

Helen Marshall supplied Prissie's wants, was introduced to her, and, standing near, joined in the talk.

Helen Marshall was very slight and graceful. Soon she piloted Prissie here and there without disturbing anyone's arrangements. At last the two girls found themselves in an immense conservatory, which opened into the drawing room at one end. Priscilla's eyes sparkled at the sight of the lovely flowers. She forgot herself and made eager exclamations of ecstasy. Helen, who up to now had thought her a dull sort of girl, began to take an interest in her.

"I'll take you into our fern house, which is just beyond here," she said. "We have got such exquisite maidenhairs and such a splendid Killarney fern."

The fern house seemed to be deserted. Helen opened the door first and ran forward. Prissie followed. A girl stood up suddenly and confronted them. The girl was Maggie Oliphant. She was sitting there alone. Her face was absolutely colorless and tears were lying wet on her eyelashes.

Maggie made a swift remark, a passing jest, and hurried past the two into the conservatory.

Priscilla could scarcely tell why, but at that moment she lost all interest in both ferns and flowers. The look of misery on Maggie's face seemed to strike her own heart like a chill.

"You look tired," said Helen Marshall, who had not noticed Maggie's tearful eyes.

"Perhaps I am," answered Prissie.

They went back again into the drawing room. Prissie still could see nothing but Miss Oliphant's eyes and the look of distress on her pale face.

Helen suddenly made a remark.

"Was there ever such a merry creature as Maggie?" she said. "Do look at her now."

Prissie raised her eyes. Miss Oliphant was the center of a gay group, among whom Geoffrey Hammond stood. Her laugh rang out clear and joyous; her smile was like sunshine, her cheeks had roses in them, and her eyes were as bright as stars.

❧XI❧

Conspirators

nnie Day and her friend Rosalind ceased to laugh as soon as they turned the corner. Annie now turned her eyes and fixed them on Rosalind, who blushed and looked uncomfortable.

"Well," said Annie, "you are a humbug, Rose! What a story you told me about Mr. Hammond—how he looked at you and was so anxious to make use of you. Oh, you know all you said. You expected a little fun for yourself, didn't you, my friend? Well, it seems to me that if anyone is to have the fun, it is Priscilla Peel."

Rosalind had rather a nervous manner. She bit her lips now; her baby-blue eyes looked angry, her innocent face wore a frown. She dropped her hold of Annie Day's arm.

Miss Day was one of the most commonplace girls at Heath Hall. She had neither good looks nor talent; she had no refinement of nature, nor had she those rugged but sterling qualities of honesty and integrity of purpose which go far to cover a multitude of other defects.

81

"I wish you wouldn't speak to me in that way," said Rosalind with a little gasp. "I hate people to laugh at me."

"Oh, no! You're such a dear little innocent baby."

"Don't, don't!" said Rosalind. "Look here, Annie, I must say something—yes, I must. I *hate* Maggie Oliphant!"

"You hate Miss Oliphant?" Annie Day turned round and stared at her companion. "When did this revolution take place, my dear? What about Rose and Maggie sitting side by side at dinner? And Rose creeping away all by herself to Maggie's room and angling for an invitation to cocoa, and trying hard, very hard, to become a member of the Dramatic Society, just because Maggie acts so splendidly. Has it not been *Maggie—Maggie*—ever since the term began, until some of us girls absolutely hated the sound of her name? Oh, Rose, what a fickle girl you are. I am ashamed of you!"

"Don't!" said Rose again. She linked her hand half timidly in Miss Day's arm. Miss Day was almost a head and shoulder above the little, delicate, fairylike creature. "I suppose I can't help changing my mind," she said. "I *did* love Maggie, of course I loved her—she fascinated me; but I don't care for her—no, I *hate* her now!"

"You must give me some reasons for this grievous change in your feelings."

"She snubbed me," said Rosalind. "She made little of me. I offered to do her a kindness and she rejected me."

"Now then, my love, let me whisper a little secret to you. I have never loved Miss Oliphant. I have never been a victim of her charms. Time was when she and Miss Lee—poor Annabel!—ruled the whole of our hall. Those two girls carried everything before them. That was before your day, Rose. Then Miss Lee died. She caught a chill, had a fever, and was dead in a couple of days. They moved her to the hospital, and she died there. Oh, there was such excitement, and such grief—even *I* was sorry; for Annabel had a way about her, I can't describe it, but she *could* fascinate you. We didn't used to think much about Maggie when Annabel was around; but now, what with Maggie and her mystery, and Maggie and her love affair, and Maggie and her handsome face and her wealth—why she bids to be more popular even than the two were when they were together.

"Yes, little Rose, I don't want her to be popular any more than you do. I hate that mawkish kind of nonsense," continued Miss Day, looking very virtuous.

Rosalind was glad that the gathering darkness prevented her sharp companion from seeing the blush on her face, for among her own sacred possessions she kept an autographed letter of Maggie's and, until the moment when all her feelings had undergone such a change, was secretly saving up her pence to buy a frame for it. Now she inquired eagerly:

"What is the mystery about Miss Oliphant? So many people hint about it, I do wish you would tell me, Annie."

"If I told you, it would cease to be a mystery."

"But you might say what you know. *Do*, Annie!"

"Well, when Annabel died, people said that Maggie had more cause than anyone else to be sorry. I never could find out what that cause was, but the servants spread some reports. They said they had found Maggie and Annabel together; Annabel had fainted, and Maggie was in an awful state of misery. Miss Heath was sent for and was a long time soothing Maggie. There was no apparent reason for this although, somehow or other, little whispers got abroad that the mystery of Annabel's illness and Maggie's distress was connected with Geoffrey Hammond.

"Of course, nothing was known, and nothing is known; but, certainly, the little whisper got into the air. Dear me, Rosalind, you need not eat me with your eyes. I am repeating mere con-jectures, and it is highly probable that not the slightest notice would have been taken of this little rumor but for the tragedy which immediately followed. Annabel, who had been as gay and well as anyone at breakfast that morning, was never seen in the college again. She was unconscious, the servants said, for a long time, and when she awoke was in high fever. She was removed to the hospital, and poor Annabel died in two days."

Rosalind was silent. After a while she said in a prim little voice, which she adopted now and then when she wanted to conceal her real feelings:

"But I do wonder what the quarrel was about—I mean, what really happened between Annabel and Maggie?"

"Look here, Rosalind, have I said anything about a quarrel? Please remember that the whole thing is conjecture from begin-ning to end, and don't go all over the place spreading stories and making mischief. I have told you this in confidence, so don't forget."

"I won't forget," replied Rosalind. "I don't know why you should accuse me of wanting to make mischief, Annie. I can't help being curious, and, of course, I'd like to know more."

"Well, for that matter, so would I," replied Annie. "Where there is a mystery it's much more satisfactory to get to the bottom of it. Of course, something dreadful must have hap-pened. It would be a comfort to know the truth, and, of course, one need never talk of it. By the way, Rosie, you are just the person to ferret this little secret out; you are the right sort of person for spying and peeping."

"Oh, thanks indeed," replied Rosalind. "If that's your opinion of me, I'm not inclined to do anything to please you. Spying and peeping! What next?"

Annie Day patted her companion's small, white hand.

"And so I've hurt the dear's feelings!" she said. "But I didn't mean to— no, that I didn't. Well, Rosie, you know what I mean. If we can find out the truth about Miss Maggie we'll just have a quiet little crow over her all to ourselves. I don't suppose we shall find out, but the opportunities may arise—who knows? Now I want to speak to you about another person, and that is Maggie's new friend."

"Poverty will be the height of the fashion, and it will be considered wrong even to go in for the recognized college recreations.

"What new friend?" Rosalind blushed slightly.

"That ugly Priscilla Peel. She has taken her up. Anyone can see that."

"Oh, I don't think so."

"But I do. Now, I have good reason not to like Miss Priscilla. You know what a virtuous parade she made of herself a few nights ago?"

"Yes, you told me."

"Horrid minx! Just the sort of girl who ought to be suppressed and crushed out of a college like ours. Flaunting her poverty in our very faces and refusing to make herself pleasant or one with us in any sort of way. Nancy Banister was in the room when Prissie made her little oration, and Nancy took her up as if she were a heroine and spoke of her as if she had done something magnificent. Of course, Nancy told Maggie, and now Maggie is as thick as possible with Prissie. So you see, my dear Rosalind—"

"I don't see—" began Rosalind.

"You little goose, before a week is out Prissie will be the fashion. All the girls will flock around her when Maggie takes her part. Bare, ugly rooms will be the rage; poverty will be the height of the fashion, and it will be considered wrong even to go in for the recognized college recreations. Rosie, my love, we must nip this growing mischief in the bud."

"How?" asked Rosalind.

"We must separate Maggie Oliphant and Priscilla Peel."

"How?" asked Rose again. "I'm sure," she added in a vehement voice, "I'm willing—I'm more than willing."

"Good. Well, we're at home now, and I absolutely must have a cup of tea. No time for it in my room tonight—let's come into the hall and have some there. Look here, Rosalind, I'll ask Lucy Marsh to have cocoa tonight in my room, and you can come too. Now keep a silent tongue in your head."

A Good Time to be Young

t was long past the tea hour at Heath Hall when Maggie Oliphant and Priscilla Peel started on their walk home. The brightness and gaiety of the merry party at the Marshalls' had increased as the moments flew on. Even Priscilla had caught something of the charm. She first became interested, then she forgot herself. Prissie was no longer awkward; she began to talk, and when she liked she could talk well.

As the two girls were leaving the house, Geoffrey Hammond put in a sudden appearance.

"I will see you home," he said to Maggie.

"No, no, you mustn't," she answered. She forgot Prissie's presence and half turned her back on her.

"How unkind you are!" said the young man in a low tone.

"No, Geoffrey, but I am struggling—you don't know how hard I am struggling—to be true to myself."

"You are altogether mistaken in your idea of truth," said Hammond, turning and walking a little way by her side.

"I am not mistaken—I am right."

"Well, at least allow me to explain my side of the question."

"No, I am resolved. Good night, you must not come any further."

She held out her hand. Hammond took it limply between his own.

"You are very cruel," he murmured in the lowest of voices.

He raised his hat, forgot even to bow to Priscilla, and hurried off down a side street.

Maggie walked on a little way. Then she turned and looked down the street where he had vanished. Suddenly she raised her hand to her lips, kissed it, and blew the kiss after the figure who had already disappeared.

Prissie, standing miserable and forgotten by the tall, handsome girl's side, could see the light in her eyes and the glow on her cheeks in the lamplight.

"I am here," said Priscilla at last in a low, half-frightened voice. "I am sorry I am here, but I am. I heard what you said to Mr. Hammond. I am sorry I heard."

Maggie turned slowly and looked at her. Prissie returned her gaze. Then, as if further words were wrung from her against her will, she continued:

"I saw the tears in your eyes in the fern house at the Marshalls'. I am very sorry, but I did see them."

"My dear Prissie!" said Maggie. She went up suddenly to the girl, put her arm round her neck, and kissed her.

"Come home now," she said, drawing Prissie's hand through her arm. "I don't think I greatly mind your knowing," she said after a pause. "You are true; I see it in your face. You would never tell—you would never make mischief."

"Tell! Of course not." Prissie's words came out with great vigor.

"I know you would not, Priscilla; may I call you Priscilla?"

"Yes."

"Will you be my friend and shall I be your friend?"

"If you would," said Prissie. "But you don't mean it. It is impossible that you can mean it. I'm not a bit like you—and—and—you only say these things to be kind."

"What do you mean, Priscilla?"

"I must tell you," said Prissie, turning very pale. "I heard what you said to Miss Banister the night I came to the college."

"You could not expect me to fall in love with you the moment I saw you."

"What I said to Miss Banister? What did I say?"

"Oh, can't you remember? The words seemed burnt into me; I shall never forget them. I had left my purse in the dining hall, and I was going to fetch it. Your door was a little open. I heard my name, and I stopped—yes, I did stop to listen."

"Oh, what a naughty, mean little Prissie! You stopped to listen. And what did you hear? Nothing good, of course? The bad thing was said to punish you for listening."

"I heard," said Priscilla, her own cheeks crimson now, "I heard you say that it gave you a passing pleasure to be kind, and that was why you were good to me."

Maggie felt her own color rising.

"Well, my dear," she said, "it still gives me an amusing pleasure to be kind. You could not expect me to fall in love with you the moment I saw you. I was kind to you then, perhaps, for the reason I stated. It is very different now."

"It was wrong of you to be kind to me for that reason."

"Wrong of me? What an extraordinary girl you are, Priscilla—why was it wrong of me?"

"Because my whole heart went out to you when you were so sweet and gentle and kind. You spoke courteously when others were rude and only laughed. I did not think—I could not possibly think—that you were good just because it gave you a sort of selfish pleasure. When I heard your words, I felt dreadful. I hated St. Benet's; I wished I had never come. Your words turned everything to bitterness for me."

"Did they really, Priscilla? Oh, Prissie! What a thoughtless, wild, impulsive creature I am. Well, I don't feel now as I did that night. If those words were cruel, forgive me. Forget those words, Prissie."

"I will if you will."

"I? I have forgotten them utterly."

"Thank you, thank you."

"Then we'll be friends—real friends, true friends?"

"Yes."

"That is right. Now keep your hand in my arm. Let's walk fast. Is it not glorious to walk in this semi-frosty sort of weather? Prissie, you'll see a vast lot that you don't approve of in your new friend."

"Oh, I don't care," said Priscilla.

She felt so joyous she could have skipped.

"I've as many sides," continued Maggie, "as a chameleon has colors. I am the gayest of the gay, as well as the saddest of the sad. When I am gay you may laugh with me, but, I warn you, when I am sad you must never cry with me. Leave me alone when I have my dark moods on, Prissie."

"Very well, Maggie, I'll remember."

"I think you'll make a delightful friend," said Maggie, glancing at Priscilla, "but I pity your side of the bargain."

"Why?"

"Because I'll try you so fearfully."

"Oh, no, you won't. I don't want to have a perfect friend."

"Perfect. No, child—heaven forbid. But there are shades of perfection. Now, when I get into my dark moods, I feel wicked as well as sad. No, we won't talk of them; we'll keep them away. Prissie, I feel good tonight—good—and glad."

"I am sure of it," said Priscilla.

"What do you know about it? You have not tasted life yet. Wait until you do. For instance—no, though—I won't enlighten you. Prissie, what do you think of Geoffrey Hammond?"

"I think he loves you very much."

"Poor Geoffrey! Now, Prissie, you are to keep that little thought quite dark in your mind—in fact, you are to put it out of your mind. You are not to associate my name with Mr. Hammond's—not even in your thoughts. You will very likely hear us spoken of together, and some of the stupid girls here will make senseless remarks. But there will be no truth in them, Prissie. He is nothing to me nor I to him."

"Then why did you blow a kiss after him?" asked Priscilla.

Maggie stood still. It was too dark for Priscilla to see her blush.

"Oh, my many-sided nature!" she suddenly exclaimed. "It was a wicked sprite made me blow that kiss. Prissie, my dear, I am cold; race me to the house."

The two girls entered the wide hall, flushed and laughing. Other girls were lingering about on the stairs. Some were just starting off to evening service at Kingsdene; others were standing in groups, chatting. Nancy Banister came up and spoke to Maggie. Maggie took her arm and walked away with her.

Prissie found herself standing alone in the hall. It was as if the delightful friendship cemented between herself and Miss

Oliphant in the frosty air outside had fallen to pieces like a castle of cards the moment they entered the house. Her high spirits went down a very little. Then, resolving to banish the spirit of distrust, she prepared to run upstairs to her own room.

Miss Heath called her name as she was passing an open door.

"Is that you, my dear? Will you come to my room after supper tonight?"

"Oh, thank you," said Prissie, her eyes sparkling.

Miss Heath came to the threshold of her pretty room and smiled at the young girl.

"You look well and happy," she said. "You are getting at home here. You will love us all yet."

"I love you now!" said Prissie with fervor.

A rather disagreeable voice said suddenly at her back: "I beg your pardon," and Lucy Marsh ran down the stairs.

The expression on Lucy's face was unpleasant. Prissie did not notice it, however. She went slowly up to her room. The electric light was on, the fire was blazing merrily. Priscilla removed her hat and jacket, threw herself into the one easy chair the room contained, and gave herself up to pleasant dreams. Many new aspects of life were opening before her. She felt that it was a good thing to be young, and she was distinctly conscious of a great, soft glow of happiness.

§XIII§

Caught
in a Trap

 ollege life is school life over again, but with wide dif-
ferences. The restraints that characterize the existence
of a schoolgirl are scarcely felt at all by the girl graduate. There are no punishments. Up to a certain point, she is
free to be industrious or not as she pleases. In short, the young
girl graduate is no longer thought of as a child. She is a woman,
with a woman's responsibilities; she is treated accordingly.

Miss Day, Miss Marsh, and Miss Merton, however, entered
heartily into the childish little plot which should deprive
Priscilla of Maggie Oliphant's friendship. They were anxious to
succeed in this because their characters were low, their natures
jealous and mean. Prissie had set up a higher standard than
theirs. If in crushing Prissie they could also bring discredit
upon Miss Oliphant, their sense of victory would be complete.

Maggie Oliphant did not care in the least what girls like
Miss Day or Miss Marsh said or thought about her, and
Priscilla, who was very happy and industrious just now, heard
many innuendoes and sly little speeches without taking in their
meaning.

Still, the conspirators did not despair. The term before Christmas was in some ways rather a dull one, and they were glad of any excitement to break the monotony. They were resolved not to leave a stone unturned to effect their object. Where there is a will there is a way. This is true as regards evil and good things alike.

One foggy morning toward the end of November, Priscilla was standing by the door of one of the lecture rooms, a book of French history, a French grammar and exercise book, and a thick notebook in her hand. She was going to her French lecture and was standing patiently by the lecture room door, which had not yet been opened.

Priscilla's strongest bias was for Greek and Latin, but Mr. Hayes had recommended her to take up modern languages as well, and she was steadily plodding through the French and German. Prissie was a very eager learner, and she was busy now looking over her notes of the last lecture and standing close to the door, so as to be one of the first to take her place in the lecture room.

The rustling of a dress caused her to look round, and she saw Rosalind Merton standing by her side. Rosalind was by no means one of the "students" of the college. She attended as few lectures as were compatible with her remaining there, but French happened to be one of the subjects which she thought it well to take up, and she appeared now by Prissie's side.

"Isn't it cold?" she said, shivering and raising her pretty face to Priscilla's.

Prissie glanced at her for a moment, said yes, she supposed it was cold, and bent her head once more over her notebook.

Rosalind was looking very pretty in a dress of dark blue velveteen. Her golden curly hair lay in little tendrils all over her head and curled lovingly against her soft white throat. She pulled out a small gold watch, which she wore at her girdle.

"How stupid of me to have mistaken the hour!" she exclaimed. Then looking hard at Prissie, she continued in an anxious tone, "You are not going to attend any lectures this afternoon, are you, Miss Peel?"

"No," answered Priscilla. "Why?"

"I wonder—" she began. "I am so worried, I *wonder* if you'd do me a kindness."

"I can't say until you ask me," said Priscilla. "What do you want me to do?"

"There's a girl at Kingsdene, a Miss Forbes. She makes my dresses now and then. I had a letter from her last night, and she is going to London in a hurry because her mother is ill. She made this dress for me. Isn't it pretty?"

"Yes," answered Priscilla, just glancing at it. "But what connection has that with my doing anything for you?"

"Oh, a great deal. I'm coming to that part. Miss Forbes wants me to pay her for making this dress before she goes to London. I can only do this by going to Kingsdene this afternoon."

"Well?" said Priscilla.

"I want to know if you will come with me. Miss Heath does not like our going to the town alone, particularly at this time of year when the evenings are so short. Will you come with me, Miss Peel? It will be awfully good-natured of you, and I really do want poor Miss Forbes to have her money before she goes to London."

"But cannot some of your own friends go with you?" returned Priscilla. "I want to work up my Greek notes this afternoon. The next lecture is a very stiff one, and I shan't be ready for it without some hard work."

"Oh, but you can study when you come back. *Do* come with me. I would not ask you, only I know you are so good-natured, and Annie Day and Lucy Marsh both have to attend lectures this afternoon. I have no one to ask—no one, really, if you refuse. I have not half so many friends as you think."

Priscilla hesitated for a moment. Two or three other girls were walking down the corridor to the lecture room; the door was flung open.

"Very well," she said as she entered the room, followed by Rosalind, "I will go with you. At what hour do you want to start?"

"At three o'clock. I'm awfully grateful. A thousand thanks, Miss Peel."

Prissie nodded, seated herself at the lecture table, and in the interest of the work that lay before her soon forgot all about Rosalind and her troubles.

The afternoon of that day turned out not only foggy but wet. A drizzling rain shrouded the landscape, and very few girls from St. Benet's were venturing abroad.

At half past two Nancy Banister came hastily into Priscilla's room.

"Maggie and I are going down to the library," she said, "to have a cozy read by the fire; we want you to come with us. Why, surely you are not going out, Miss Peel?"

"Yes, I am," answered Prissie in a resigned voice. "I don't like it a bit, but Miss Merton has asked me to go with her to Kingsdene, and I promised."

"Well, you shan't keep your promise. This is not a fit day for you to go out, and you have a cough, too. I heard you coughing last night."

"Yes, but that is nothing. I must go, Miss Banister; I must keep my word."

"I never knew that Rosalind Merton was one of your friends, Prissie," continued Nancy in a puzzled voice.

"Nor is she—I scarcely know her. But when she asked me to go out with her, I could not very well say no."

"I suppose not. Well, come back as soon as you can. Maggie and I are going to have a jolly time, and we only wish you were with us."

Nancy nodded brightly and took her leave, and Priscilla, putting on her waterproof and her shabbiest hat, went down into the hall to meet Rosalind.

Rosalind's hat was extremely pretty and becoming, and Priscilla fancied she got a glimpse of a gay silk dress under her fur-lined coat.

"Oh, it's quite too sweet of you to be ready!" said Rosalind. She took Prissie's hand and squeezed it affectionately, and the two girls set off.

The walk was a dreary one, for Kingsdene, one of the most beautiful places in England in fine weather, lies so low that in the winter months fogs are frequent and the rain is almost incessant. By the time the two girls had got into the High Street, Prissie's thick, sensible boots were covered with mud and Rosalind's thin ones felt very damp to her feet.

They soon reached the quarter where the dressmaker, Miss Forbes, lived. Prissie was asked to wait downstairs, and Rosalind ran up several flights of stairs to fulfill her mission. She came back at the end of a few minutes looking bright and radiant.

"I am sorry to have kept you waiting, Miss Peel," she said, "but my boots were so muddy that Miss Forbes insisted on polishing them up for me."

"Well, we can go home now, I suppose?" said Prissie.

"Ye—es; only as we *are* here, would you greatly mind our going round by Bouverie Street? I want to inquire for a friend of mine, Mrs. Elliot-Smith. She has not been well."

"Oh, I don't mind," said Priscilla. "Will it take us much out of our way?"

"No, only a step or two. Come, we have just to turn this corner, and here we are. What a good-natured girl you are, Miss Peel!"

Prissie said nothing. The two started forth again in the drizzling mist and fog, and presently found themselves standing before a ponderous hall door.

Rosalind rang the bell, which made a loud peal. The door was opened almost immediately; but, instead of a servant appearing in answer to the summons, a showily-dressed girl with a tousled head of flaxen hair, light blue eyes, and a pale face stood before Rosalind and Prissie.

"Oh, you dear Rose!" she said, clasping her arms round Miss Merton and dragging her into the house. "I had almost given you up. Do come in, both of you. What a miserable, horrid, too utterly depressing afternoon it is!"

"How do you do, Meta?" said Rosalind, when she could interrupt this eager flow of words. "May I introduce my friend, Miss Peel? Miss Peel, this is my very great and special friend and chum, Meta Elliot-Smith."

"Oh, you charming darling!" said Meta, giving Rose a fresh hug and glancing in a friendly way at Prissie.

"We came to inquire for your mother, dear Meta," said Rose in a demure tone. "Is she any better?"

"Yes, my dear darling, she's much better." Meta's eyes flashed interrogation into Rose's. Rose returned glances which spoke whole volumes of meaning.

"Look here," said Meta Elliot-Smith, "now that you two dear, precious girls have come, you mustn't go away. Oh, no, I couldn't hear of it. I have perfect oceans to say to you, Rose—and it is absolutely centuries since we have met. Off with your waterproof and up you come to the drawing room for a cup of tea. One or two friends are dropping in presently, and the Beechers and one or two more are upstairs now. You know the Beechers, don't you, Rosalind? Here, Miss Peel, let me help you to unburden yourself."

Priscilla opened her eyes wide as she gazed at her companion. She saw at once that she had been trapped.

"Oh, but indeed I can't stay," said Prissie. "It is quite impossible! You know, Miss Merton, it is impossible. We are due at St. Benet's now. We ought to be going back at once."

Rosalind Merton's only answer was to slip off her coat and stand arrayed in a fascinating frock of silk and lace—a little too dressy, perhaps, even for an afternoon party at Kingsdene, but vastly becoming to its small wearer.

Priscilla opened her eyes wide as she gazed at her companion. She saw at once that she had been trapped, and that Rosalind's real object in coming to Kingsdene was not to pay her dressmaker but to visit the Elliot-Smiths.

"I can't possibly stay," she said in a cold, angry voice. "I must go back to St. Benet's at once."

She began to button up her waterproof as fast as Miss Elliot-Smith was unbuttoning it.

"Nonsense, you silly old dear!" said Rosalind, who, having gained her way, was now in the best of spirits. "You mustn't listen to her, Meta. She studies a great deal too hard, and a little relaxation will do her all the good in the world. My dear Miss Peel, you can't be so rude as to refuse a cup of tea, and I know I shall catch an awful cold if I don't have one. Do come upstairs for half an hour, dear Prissie!"

Her muddy boots were pushed far in under her chair and hidden as much as possible by her rather short dress.

Priscilla hesitated. She had no knowledge of so-called "society." Her instincts told her it was very wrong to humor Rose. She disliked Miss Elliot-Smith and felt wild at the trick that had been played on her. Nevertheless, on an occasion of this kind, she was no match for Rose.

"Just for a few moments," said Rosalind, coming up and whispering to her. "I really won't keep you long. You *will* just oblige me for a few minutes."

"Well, but I'm not fit to be seen in this old dress!" whispered back poor Prissie.

"Oh, yes, you are. You're not bad at all, and I am sure Meta will find you a secluded corner if you want it—won't you, Meta?"

"Yes, of course, if Miss Peel wants it," answered Meta. "But she looks all right, so deliciously quaint—I simply *adore* quaint people! Quite the sweet girl graduate, I do declare!"

So Prissie, in her ill-made brown dress, her shabbiest hat, and her muddy boots, had to follow in the wake of Rosalind Merton and her friend. At first she had been too angry to think much about her attire, but she was painfully conscious of it when she entered a crowded drawing room where everyone else was in suitable afternoon attire. She was glad to shrink away out of sight into the most remote corner she could find; her muddy boots were pushed far in under her chair and hidden as much as possible by her rather short dress.

It was in vain for poor Priscilla to whisper to herself that Greek and Latin were glorious and great and dress and fashion were things of no moment whatever. At this instant she knew all too well that dress and fashion were reigning supreme.

Meta Elliot-Smith was effusive, loud, and vulgar, but she was also good-natured. She admired Rosalind, but in her heart of hearts she thought that her friend had played Prissie a very shabby trick. She brought Prissie some tea, therefore, and stood for a moment or two by her side, trying to make things a little more comfortable for her. Someone soon claimed her attention, however, and poor Prissie found herself alone.

❧XIV❧

In the Elliot-Smiths' Drawing Room

he fun and talk rose fast and furious. More and more guests arrived; the large drawing rooms were soon full. Priscilla, from her corner, half hidden by a sheltering window curtain, looked in vain for Rosalind. Where had she hidden herself? Surely Rosalind would come to fetch her soon. They had to walk home and be ready for dinner.

Dinner at St. Benet's was at half past six, and Prissie reflected with a great sensation of thankfulness that Rosalind and she must go back in good time for this meal, as it was one of the rules of the college that no girl should be absent from dinner without getting permission from the principal.

Prissie looked in agony at the clock that stood on a mantelpiece not far from where she had ensconced herself. Presently it struck five; no one heard its silver note in the babel of sound, but Priscilla watched its slowly moving hands in agony. She reflected, to her horror, that she had not the moral courage to walk about those drawing rooms hunting for Rose.

Two or three exquisitely-dressed but frivolous-looking women stood in a group not far from the window where Priscilla sat.

They talked about the price they had paid for their new winter bonnets. Their shrill laughter reached Prissie's ear, as did their words. They complimented one another, but talked scandal of their neighbors. They called somebody—who Prissie could not imagine—"a certain lady," and spoke of how she was angling to get a footing in society, and how the good set at Kingsdene would certainly never have anything to do with her or hers.

"She's taking up those wretched girl graduates," said one of these gossips to her neighbor. Then her eye fell upon Prissie. She said "Hush!" in an audible tone, and the little party moved away out of earshot.

The minute hand of the clock on the mantelpiece pointed to nearly half past five. Poor Prissie felt that, in addition to having lost so many hours of study, she would get into a serious scrape at St. Benet's for breaking one of the known rules of the college.

At this moment a quiet voice said, "How do you do?"

She raised her eyes. Geoffrey Hammond was standing by her side. He gave her a kind glance, shook hands with her, and then, dropping into a nearby chair, he said abruptly, "I saw you from the other end of the room. I was surprised. I did not suppose you knew our hostess."

"Nor do I really," said Priscilla. "Oh, it's a shame!" she added, her face reddening up woefully. "I have been trapped!"

"You must not let the people who are near us hear you say words of that kind," said Hammond. "They will crowd around to hear your story. Now, I want it all to myself. Do you think you can tell it to me in a low voice?"

To poor Hammond's horror, Prissie began to whisper.

"I beg your pardon," he said, interrupting her, "but do you know that the buzzing noise caused by a whisper carries sound

103

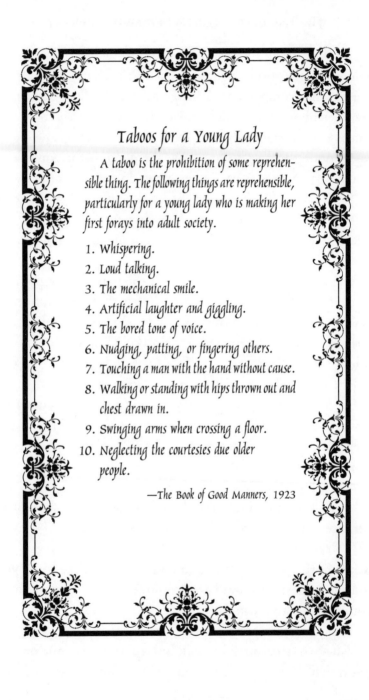

Taboos for a Young Lady

A taboo is the prohibition of some reprehensible thing. The following things are reprehensible, particularly for a young lady who is making her first forays into adult society.

1. Whispering.
2. Loud talking.
3. The mechanical smile.
4. Artificial laughter and giggling.
5. The bored tone of voice.
6. Nudging, patting, or fingering others.
7. Touching a man with the hand without cause.
8. Walking or standing with hips thrown out and chest drawn in.
9. Swinging arms when crossing a floor.
10. Neglecting the courtesies due older people.

—The Book of Good Manners, 1923

a long way? That is a well-authenticated fact. Now, if you will try to speak low."

"Oh, thank you. Yes, I will," said Prissie. She began a garbled account. At last he ascertained that Priscilla's all-absorbing present anxiety was to be in time for the half-past-six dinner at St. Benet's.

"I know we'll be late," she said, "and I'll have broken the rules, and Miss Heath will be so much annoyed with me."

Hammond volunteered to look for Miss Merton.

"Oh, thank you," said Prissie. "How very, very kind you are."

"Please don't speak of it," said Hammond. "Stay where you are. I'll soon bring the young truant to your side."

He began to move about the drawing rooms, and Prissie watched him from her hiding place with a world of gratitude in her face. "Now I do hope Mr. Hammond will find Miss Merton quickly. How kind he is! I wonder why Maggie does not care for him as much as he cares for her. I do not feel half as shy with him as I do with everyone else in this dreadful, dreadful room."

Hammond was absent about ten minutes. To her horror she saw him returning alone, and now she so far forgot her muddy boots as to run two or three steps to meet him. She knocked over a footstool as she did so, and one or two people looked round and shrugged their shoulders at the poor clumsy girl.

"Where is she?" exclaimed Prissie, again speaking in a loud voice.

"It's all right, I assure you, Miss Peel. Let me conduct you back to that snug seat in the window. I have seen Miss Merton, and she says you are to make yourself happy. She asked Miss Heath's permission for you both to be absent from dinner today."

"She did? I never heard of anything so outrageous. I won't stay."

"I am not supposed to know the ways of society," she said, "but I don't think I want to know much about this sort of society."

"Had you not better just think calmly over it? If you return to St. Benet's without Miss Merton, will you get her into a scrape?"

"Do you think I care? Oh, she has behaved disgracefully!"

Priscilla was not often in a passion, but she felt in one now. She lost her shyness, and her voice rose without constraint.

"I am not supposed to know the ways of society," she said, "but I don't think I want to know much about this sort of society." And she got up, prepared to leave the room.

The ladies who had been gossiping at her side turned at the sound of her agitation. They saw a plain, badly-dressed girl standing up and contradicting, or at least appearing to contradict, Geoffrey Hammond, one of the best-known men at St. Hilda's, a Senior Wrangler, too. What did this girl mean? Most people were deferential to Hammond, but she seemed to be scolding him.

Prissie, for the time being, became more interesting than even the winter fashions. The ladies drew a step or two nearer to enjoy the little comedy.

Priscilla noticed no one, but Hammond's cheeks burned and he wished himself well out of his present position.

"If you will sit down, Miss Peel," he said in a low, firm voice, "I think I can give you good reasons for not rushing away in this headlong fashion."

"Well, what are they?" said Prissie. Hammond's voice had a sufficiently compelling power to make her sit down once more.

"Don't you think," he said, seating himself in front of her, "that we may as well keep this discussion to ourselves?"

"Oh, yes. Was I speaking too loud? I wouldn't vex *you* for anything."

"Pardon me. You are still speaking a little loud."

"Oh!" Poor Prissie fell back, her face crimson. "Please say anything you wish," she presently piped in a voice as low as a little mouse might have used.

"What I have to say is simply this," said Hammond. "You will gain nothing now by rushing off to St. Benet's. However hard you struggle, you cannot get there in time for dinner. Would it not be best, then, to remain here quietly until Miss Merton asks you to accompany her back to the college?"

"Thank you. Perhaps that is best. It is quite hopeless now to think of getting back in time for dinner. I only hope Miss Merton won't keep me waiting very long, for it is very, very dull sitting here and seeing people staring at you."

"I would not look at them if I were you, Miss Peel. And, if you will permit me, I shall be only too pleased to keep you company."

"Oh, thank you," said Prissie. "Then I shan't mind staying at all."

The next half hour seemed to pass on the wings of the wind.

Priscilla was engaged in an animated discussion with Hammond on the relative attractions of the *Iliad* and the *Odyssey*; her opinion differed from his, and she was well able to hold her ground. Her face was now both eloquent and attractive, her eyes were bright. She looked so different a girl from the cowed and miserable little Prissie of an hour ago that Rosalind Merton, as she came up and tapped her on the shoulder, felt a pang of envy.

"I am sorry to interrupt you," she said, "but it is time for us to be going home. Have you given Mr. Hammond his message?"

"What do you mean?" asked Priscilla. "I have not any message for Mr. Hammond."

"You must have forgotten. Did not Miss Oliphant give you a letter for him?"

"Certainly not. What do you mean?"

"I felt sure I saw her," said Rosalind. "I suppose I was mistaken. Well, sorry as I am to interrupt a pleasant talk, I fear I must ask you to come home with me now."

She raised her pretty baby-blue eyes to Hammond's face as she spoke. He absolutely scowled down at her, shook hands warmly with Priscilla, and turned away.

"Come and bid Mrs. Elliot-Smith good-bye," said Rosalind, her eyes still dancing. "She is at the other end of the drawing room."

"How disgracefully you have behaved, Miss Merton!" began Priscilla at once. "You cannot expect me ever to speak to you again."

They were walking across the crowded drawing room now. Rosalind turned and let her laughing eyes look full at Prissie.

"My dear Miss Peel, pray reserve any little scolding you intend to bestow upon me until we get out into the street, and please do not tread upon my dress!"

❧XV❧

Polly Singleton

iss Day was having quite a large party for cocoa in her room. She had invited not only her own chosen friends from Heath Hall, but also two or three congenial spirits from Katharine Hall. Miss Day's room was one of the largest in the college; it was showily furnished with an intention to produce a Japanese effect. Several paper lanterns hung from the ceiling and were suspended on wire supports, which were fastened to different articles of furniture.

The lanterns were all lit now, and Miss Day thought her room lovely. It was dazzling but the reverse of soothing.

The girls were lounging about, chatting and laughing. One, a red-haired girl, with frank, open blue eyes and a freckled face—an inmate of Katharine Hall—was sending her companions into fits of laughter.

"Yes," she was saying in a high, gay voice, "There's never the least use in not owning the truth. I'm used up, girls; I haven't a pennypiece to bless myself with, and this letter came from Spilman tonight. Spilman says he'll see Miss Eccleston if I don't pay up. Madame Clarice wrote two nights ago, declaring *her* intention of visiting Miss Eccleston if I didn't send her some money. I shall have no money until next term. There's a state of affairs!"

"What do you mean to do, Polly?" asked Lucy Marsh in a sympathizing tone.

"Do? My dear creature, there's only one thing to be done. I must have an auction on the quiet. I shall sell my worldly all. I can buy things again, you know, after dad sends me his next allowance."

"Oh, Polly, but you cannot really mean it!" Miss Marsh, Miss Day, and two or three more crowded around Polly Singleton as they spoke.

"You can't mean to have an auction," began Miss Day. "No one ever heard of such a thing at St. Benet's. Why, it would be simply disgraceful!"

"No, it wouldn't—don't turn cross, Annie. I'll have an auction first and then a great feed in the empty room."

"But, Polly, if you write to your father, he'll be sure to send you what you want to clear off those two debts. You have often told us he has lots of money."

"My dears, he has more tin than he knows what to do with; but do you think I am going to have the poor old dear worried? When I was coming here he said, 'Polly, you shall have thirty pounds every term to spend as pocket money; not a penny more, not a penny less. And you must keep out of debt on it.' I gave the dear old dad a hug. He's the image of me—only with redder hair and more freckles. And I said, 'I'll do my best, dad. Anyhow, you shan't be put out whatever happens.'"

"Then you didn't tell him you'd keep out of debt?"

"No, for I knew I'd break my word. I've been in debt ever since I could remember. I wouldn't know how it felt not to owe a lot of money. It's habit, and I don't mind it a bit. But I don't want dad to know, and I don't want Miss Eccleston to know, for perhaps she would write to him. If those old horrors won't wait for their money till next term, why there's nothing for it but an auction. I have some nice things and they'll go very cheap, so there's a chance for you all, girls."

"But if Miss Eccleston finds out?" said Miss Day.

"What if she does? There's no rule against auctions, and, as I don't suppose any of you will have one, it isn't worth making a rule for me alone. Anyhow, I'm resolved to risk it. My auction will be on Monday, and I shall make out an inventory of my goods tomorrow."

"Will you advertise it on the notice board in your hall, dear?" asked Lucy Marsh.

"Why not? A good idea! *The great auction will be held in Miss Singleton's room, from eight to ten o'clock on the evening of Monday next. Great bargains! Enormous sacrifice! Things absolutely given away!* Oh, what fun! I'll be my own auctioneer."

Polly lay back in her armchair and laughed loudly.

"What is all this noise about?" asked a refined little voice, and Rosalind Merton entered the room.

Two or three girls jumped up at once to greet her.

"Come in, Rosie, you're just in time. What *do* you think Miss Singleton is going to do now?"

"I can't tell. What?" asked Rosalind.

"Well, my dear, there's nothing for those in debt but to sell their possessions. My auction is on Monday. Will you come, Rosalind?"

"You don't mean it," said Rose, her blue eyes beginning to sparkle.

"Yes, I do absolutely and truly mean it."

"And you will sell your things—your lovely things?"

"My things, my lovely, lovely things must be sold."

"But not your clothes? Your new sealskin jacket, for instance?"

Polly made a wry face for a moment. Putting her hand into her pocket, she pulled out Spilman's and Madame Clarice's two bills.

"I owe a lot," she said, looking at the sum total. "Yes, I even fear the sealskin must go. I don't want to part with it. Dad gave it to me just before I came here."

"It's a lovely seal," said Annie Day, "and it seems a sin to part with it."

"Don't praise it, please," said Polly, lying back in her chair and covering her eyes with her hand. "It cuts like a knife to part with dad's last present. Well, I'm rightly punished. What a fool I was to get all those Japanese things from Spilman and that fancy ball dress for the theatricals. Oh, dear! Oh, dear!"

"I know what I want," said a girl called Hetty Jones who had not yet spoken. "I'm going in for some of Polly's ornaments. You won't put too big a price upon your corals, will you, Poll?"

"I shall bid for your American rocking chair, Polly," exclaimed Miss Day.

"I tell you what you must do, Miss Singleton!" shouted another girl. "You must get those inventories ready as soon as possible and send them around the college for everyone to read, for you have got such nice things that there will be sure to be a great rush at your auction."

"I had some fun today," said Rosalind, when each of the girls, provided with their own cups of cocoa, sat round and began to sip. "I took Miss Propriety to town with me."

"Oh, did you, darling? Do tell us about it!" said Annie Day.

"There isn't much to tell. She behaved as I expected. We went to the Elliot-Smiths'," continued Rosalind.

"As long as I live I shall hate the letter P," suddenly interrupted Annie Day, "for since that disagreeable girl has got into the house we are always using it."

"Good gracious, Rosie!" interrupted Hetty Jones. "You don't mean to say you took Propriety to *that* house?"

"Yes, why not? It's the jolliest house in Kingsdene."

"But fancy taking poor Propriety there. What did she say?"

"Say? She scolded a good deal."

"Scolded! Poor little proper thing! How I should have liked to have seen her. Did she open her purse and exhibit its emptiness to the company at large? Did she stand on a chair and lecture the frivolous people who assemble in that house on the emptiness of life? Oh, how I wish I could have looked on at the fun!"

"They were so delighted with one another that I could scarcely get Prissie away when it was time to leave."

"You'd have beheld an edifying sight then, my dear," said Rosalind. "Prissie's whole behavior was one to be copied. No words can describe her tact and grace."

"But what did she do, Rosie? I wish you would speak out and tell us. You know you are keeping something back."

"Whenever she saw me she scolded me, and she tripped over my dress several times."

"Oh, you dear, good, patient Rosalind, what a bore she must have been."

"No, she wasn't, for I scarcely saw anything of her. She amused herself capitally without me, I can tell you."

"Amused herself? Propriety amused herself? Could she stoop to it?"

"She did. She stooped and—conquered. She secured for herself an adorer."

"Rosalind, how absurd you are! Poor, Plain Propriety!"

"As long as I live I shall hate the letter P," suddenly interrupted Annie Day, "for since that disagreeable girl has got into the house, we are always using it."

"Never mind, Rosalind. Go on with your story," said Miss Jones. "What did Plain Propriety do?"

Rosalind threw up her hands, rolled her eyes skyward, and uttered the terse remark: "She flirted!"

"Oh, Rosie! Who would flirt with her?"

This remark came from Lucy Marsh. Rosalind Merton, who was leaning her fair head against a dark velvet cushion, looked as if she enjoyed the situation immensely.

"What do you say to a Senior Wrangler?" she asked in a gentle voice.

"Rosalind, what—not *the* Senior Wrangler?"

Rosalind nodded. "Oh! oh! oh! What could he see in her? Geoffrey Hammond, of all people! He's so exclusive."

"Well," said Hetty Jones, standing up reluctantly, for she felt it was time to return to her neglected studies, "wonders will never cease! I could not have supposed that Mr. Hammond would condescend to go near the Elliot-Smiths', and most certainly I should never have guessed that he would look at a girl like Priscilla Peel."

"Well, he flirted with her," said Rosalind, "and she with him. They were so delighted with one another that I could scarcely get Prissie away when it was time to leave. They looked quite engrossed—you know the kind of air—there was no mistaking it!"

"Miss Peel must have thanked you for taking her."

"Thanked me? That's not Miss Prissie's style."

"Well, it's rather shabby," said Polly Singleton. "Everyone at St. Benet's knows to whom Mr. Hammond belongs."

"Yes, yes, of course, of course," cried several voices.

"And Maggie has been so kind to Miss Peel," continued Polly.

"Yes—shame!—How mean of little Propriety!" the voices echoed again.

Rosalind gave a glance at Annie Day. Annie raised her eyebrows, looked interrogative, then her face subsided into a satisfied expression. She asked no further questions, but she gave Rosalind an affectionate pat on the shoulder.

❧XVI❧

Pretty
Little Rosalind

 have done it now," said Rosalind. "The estrangement will come about naturally. My dear girls, we need do nothing further. The friendship we regretted is at an end."

"Did you take Priscilla Peel to the Elliot-Smiths' on purpose, then?" asked Miss Day.

"I took her there for my own purposes," replied Rosalind. "I wanted to go. I could not go alone, as it is against our precious rules. It was not convenient for any of my own special friends to come with me, so I thought I'd play Prissie a nice little trick. Oh, wasn't she angry! My dear girls, it was as good as a play to watch her face."

Rosalind lay back in her chair and laughed heartily. Her laughter was as melodious as the sound of silver bells.

"Well," said Miss Marsh after a pause, "I wish you would stop laughing and go on with your story, Rose."

"That's all," she said. "There's nothing more to tell."

"Did you know, then, that Mr. Hammond would be there?"

"No, I had not the least idea that piece of luck would fall my way. Meta managed that for me most delightfully. Meta got to know Mr. Hammond at a tennis party in the summer, and when she met him last week she asked him to come to her house today. All of a sudden it flashed into her head to say, 'Some of our friends from St. Benet's will be present.' The moment she said this he got very polite and said he would certainly look in for a little while. Poor Meta was so delighted! You can fancy her disappointment when he devoted himself all the time to Prissie."

"He thought he'd meet Maggie Oliphant," said Annie Day; "it was a shame to lure him on with a falsehood."

"My dear," responded Rosalind, "Meta did not tell a lie. I never could have guessed that you were strait-laced, Annie."

"Nor am I," responded Annie with a sigh, which she quickly suppressed.

"The whole thing fitted in admirably with our wishes," continued Rose, "and now we need not do anything further in the matter. Rumor, in the shape of Hetty Jones' tongue and Polly Singleton's hints, will do the rest for us."

"Do you really think that Maggie Oliphant cares for Mr. Hammond?" asked Lucy Marsh.

"Cares for him!" said Rosalind. "Does a duck swim? Does a baby like sweet things? Maggie is so much in love with Mr. Hammond that she's almost ill about it—there!"

"Nonsense!" exclaimed the other two girls.

"She is, I know she is. She treats him shamefully because of some whim of hers. I only wish she may never get him."

"He'd do nicely for you, wouldn't he, Rose?" said Annie Day.

A delicate pink came into Rosalind's cheeks. She stood to leave the room.

"Mr. Hammond is not in my style," she said. "Much too severe and too learned. Good night, girls. I must look over the notes of that wretched French lecture before I go to bed."

Rosalind sought her own room, which was in another corridor. It was late now—past eleven o'clock. The electric light had been put out. She was well-supplied with candles, however. Lighting two on the mantelpiece and two on her bureau, she proceeded to stir up her fire and to make her room warm and cozy.

Raising her white wrapper so as to get a peep at her small, pretty feet, she waltzed slowly and gracefully in front of the mirror.

Rosalind still wore the pretty, light silk which had given her such an elegant appearance at the Elliot-Smiths' that afternoon. Securing the bolt of her door, she pushed aside a heavy curtain, which concealed the part of her room devoted to her wardrobe. Rosalind's wardrobe had a glass door and she could see her petite figure in it from head to foot. It was a very small figure but exquisitely proportioned. Its owner admired it much. She took up a hand-glass and surveyed herself in profile. Then, taking off her pretty dress, she arrayed herself in a long white muslin dressing robe, and letting down her golden hair, combed out the glittering masses. They fell in showers to below her waist. Her face looked more babyish and innocent than ever as it smiled to its own fair image in the glass.

"How he did scowl at me!" said Rosalind, suddenly speaking aloud. "But I did not do badly today. I enjoyed myself and I took a nice rise out of that disagreeable Miss Peel. Now *must* I look through those horrid French notes? Need I?" She pirouetted on one toe in front of the glass. The motion exhilarated her, and, raising her white wrapper so as to get a peep at her small, pretty feet, she waltzed slowly and gracefully in front of the mirror.

"I can't and won't study tonight," she said again. "I hate study, and I will not spoil my looks by burning the midnight oil."

Suddenly she clasped her hands and the color rushed into her cheeks. "How fortunate that I remembered! I must write to mother this very night. This is Thursday. The auction is on Monday. I have not a post to lose."

Hastily seating herself in front of her bureau, Rosalind scribbled a few lines:

"DEAREST, PRECIOUS MAMSIE: Whatever happens, please send me a postal order for £10 by return. One of the richest girls in the place is going to have an auction, and I shall pick up some *treasures*. If you could spare £15, or even £20, the money would be well spent, but ten at least I must have. There is a sealskin jacket, which cost at least eighty pounds, and *such* coral ornaments—you know, that lovely pink shade. Send me all you can, precious mamsie, and make your Baby happy.

"Your own little ROSE.

"P.S.—Oh, mamsie, *such* a sealskin! and *such* coral!"

This artless epistle was quickly enclosed in an envelope, addressed, and deposited in the post-box. Afterward, pretty little Rosalind spent a night of dreamless slumber and awoke in the morning as fresh and innocent looking as the fairest of the babies she compared herself to.

Sealskin
and Pink Coral

n her walk home, Priscilla made up her mind to have nothing further to say to Rose, but also not to make a complaint about her.

Maggie and Nancy asked her casually what had kept her out so long.

"I was at the Elliot-Smiths' with Miss Merton," replied Priscilla.

They both started when she said this and looked at her hard. They were too well-mannered, however, to give utterance to the many comments that crowded to their lips. Prissie read their thoughts like a book.

"I did not like it at all," she said. "But I'd rather say nothing about it, please. After Mr. Hammond came, I was happy."

"Mr. Hammond was there?" said Nancy in an eager voice. "Geoffrey Hammond was at the Elliot-Smiths'? Impossible!"

"He was there," repeated Prissie. She glanced nervously at Maggie, who had taken up a book and was pretending to read. "He came and he spoke to me. He was very, very kind, and he made me so happy."

"Dear Prissie," said Maggie suddenly. She got up, went over to the young girl, tapped her affectionately on the shoulder, and left the room.

Prissie sat, looking thoughtfully before her. After a time she bade Nancy Banister "good night" and went off to her own room to study the notes she had taken that morning at the French lecture.

The next few days passed without anything special occurring. If a little rumor were already beginning to swell in the air, it scarcely reached the ears of those principally concerned.

Monday arrived. It was now less than three weeks to the end of the term. A good many of the girls were talking about home and Christmas, including Priscilla.

In short, things were going well with her, and she owned to her own heart that she had never felt happier in her life. Every day her friends found fresh points of interest in this queer girl. Nancy Banister was really attached to her, Maggie was most faithful in her declared friendship, and the different lecturers spoke highly of Miss Peel's comprehension, knowledge, and ability.

Under Maggie's advice, she became a member of the Debating Society and rather reluctantly allowed her name to be entered in the Dramatic Club. She felt very shy about this, but, to her astonishment, Priscilla found that she could act. If the part suited her she could throw herself into it so that she ceased to be awkward, ungainly Priscilla Peel.

The members of the society intended to act *The Princess* before the end of the term, and as there was a great deal to work up and many rehearsals were necessary, they met in the little theater on most evenings. Maggie Oliphant had been unanimously selected to take the part of the Princess.

She electrified everyone by drawing Miss Peel toward her and saying in an emphatic voice, "You must be the Prince, Priscilla."

A look of dismay crept over several faces. One or two made different proposals.

"Would not Nancy Banister take the part better, Maggie?" said Miss Claydon, a tall, graceful girl who was to be Psyche.

When she spoke to Maggie she felt no longer like a feeble schoolgirl acting a part. She imagined she was pleading for Hammond . . .

"No, Nancy is to be Cyril. She sings well and can do the part admirably. Miss Peel must be the Prince. I will have no other lover. What do you say, Miss Peel?"

"I cannot. It is impossible," almost whispered Prissie.

"'Cannot' is a word that must not be listened to in our Dramatic Society," responded Maggie. "I promise to turn you into a most accomplished Prince, my friend. Girls, do you leave this matter in my hands? Do you leave the Prince to me?"

"We cannot refuse you the privilege of choosing your own Prince, Princess," said Miss Claydon with a graceful curtsy.

The others assented, but unwillingly.

Rosalind Merton was not a particularly good actress, but her face was too pretty not to be called on. She was to take the part of Melissa.

The society had a grand meeting on the day of Polly Singleton's auction. Matters were still very much in a state of chaos, but the rehearsal of some of the parts was got through.

Priscilla had learned her speeches accurately. When her turn came, she stood up, trembling, and began. Gradually the look on Maggie's face moved her. She fancied herself Hammond, not the Prince. When she spoke to Maggie she felt no longer like a feeble schoolgirl acting a part. She thought she was pleading for Hammond, and enthusiasm got into her voice and a light filled her eyes. There was a little cheer when Priscilla got through her first rehearsal.

Nancy Banister came up to Rosalind. "I do believe Maggie is right," she said, "and that Miss Peel will play the part with talent."

"Miss Oliphant is well-known for her forgiving spirit," retorted Rosalind, an ugly look spoiling the expression of her face.

"What do you mean, Rose?"

"To choose *that* girl for her Prince!" retorted Rosalind. "Ask Mr. Hammond what I mean. Ask the Elliot-Smiths."

"I don't know the Elliot-Smiths," said Nancy in a cold voice. She turned away.

Rose glanced after her. Then she ran up to Maggie Oliphant, who was preparing to leave the little theater.

"Don't you want to see the auction?" she said in a gay voice. "It's going to be the best fun we have had for many a long day."

Maggie turned and looked at her.

"The auction? What auction do you mean?" she asked.

"Why, Polly Singleton's, of course. You've not heard of it? It's *the* event of the term!"

Maggie laughed.

"You must be talking nonsense, Rose," she said. "An auction at St. Benet's! A real auction? Impossible!"

"No, it's not impossible. It's true. Polly owes for a lot of things, and she's going to pay for them in that way. Did you not get a notice? Polly declared she would send one without fail to every girl in the college."

"Now I remember," said Miss Oliphant, laughing. "I got an extraordinary typewritten production. I regarded it as a hoax and consigned it to the wastepaper basket."

"But it wasn't a hoax. Come away, Miss Oliphant, do. Polly has got some lovely things."

"I don't think I even know who Polly is," said Maggie.

"You must know her by sight, at least. A great big, fat girl with red hair and freckles."

"Yes, now I remember. I think she has rather a pleasant face."

"You'll come to her auction?" insisted Rose.

"I don't know. She has no right to have an auction. Such a proceeding would give great displeasure to our principals."

"How can you tell that? There never was an auction at the college before."

"How can I tell, Rose? Instinct is my guide in a matter of this sort. I hope you may be successful. Good night."

Maggie turned to walk away. She saw Priscilla standing not far off.

"Come, Prissie," she said affectionately, "you did admirably tonight, but you must have another lesson. You missed two of the best points in that last speech. Come back with me into the theater at once."

Rose bit her lip with vexation. She was wildly anxious to be at the auction. The sealskin might be put up for sale with she not present. The corals might go to some other happy girl; but she had made a resolve to bring some of the very best girls in the college to this scene. Her reckless companions had dared her to do this, and she felt what she called "her honor" at stake. Nancy Banister had declined her invitation. Now she *must* secure Maggie.

"I wish you'd come," she said, following Maggie and Prissie to the door of the theater. "It will be an awful disappointment if you don't! We all reckoned on having you."

"What *do* you mean, Rose?"

"We thought you wouldn't be above a bit of fun. You never used to be, you know. You never used to be strict and proper and over-righteous."

Priscilla was startled to see the queer change these few words made upon Maggie. Her cheeks lost their roses; her eyes grew big. Then a defiant expression filled them.

"If you put it in that way," she said, "I'll go and peep at the thing. It isn't my taste nor my style, but goodness knows I'm no better than the rest of you. Come, Prissie."

Maggie seized Priscilla's hand; her clasp was so tight as to be almost painful. She hurried Prissie along so fast that Rose could scarcely keep up with them. A moment or two later they had reached the scene of the evening's amusement.

Loud voices and laughter greeted them. The atmosphere here was hot and stifling and chaos reigned supreme. Pictures and ornaments of all kinds had been removed roughly and hastily from the walls; clothes and even jewels were piled on the tables.

When Maggie, Rose, and Priscilla entered the room, Polly was exhibiting the charms of a yellow silk dress somewhat the worse for wear. Laughter choked her voice, and her bright blue eyes shone with excitement and amusement.

"Who'll try this?" she began. "It has a double charm. Not only has it graced this fair and lovely form, but the silk of which it is made was given to me by my mother's aunt, who had it from her mother before her. When I part with this, I part with a relic. Those who purchase it secure for themselves a piece of history. Who will buy, who will buy, who will buy? An historical dress going—such a bargain! Who, who will buy?"

"I'll give you five shillings, Polly," screamed a dark-eyed girl who stood near.

"Five shillings! This lovely dress going for five shillings!" proceeded Polly.

"And sixpence," added another voice.

"This beautiful, historical robe going for five-and-sixpence," said Miss Singleton in her gay voice. "Oh, it's a bargain—it's dirt cheap! Who will buy? Who will buy?"

The bids went up, and finally the yellow dress was sold to a rosy-faced country girl for the sum of thirteen shillings and ninepence.

Polly's various other possessions were one by one brought to the hammer, some of them fetching fairly large sums, for most of them were worth having, and there were wealthy girls at the college who were not above securing a bargain when it came their way.

At last the prize on which all Rose's hopes were set was put up for sale. Polly's magnificent sealskin jacket was held aloft and displayed to the admiring and covetous gaze of many. Rose's face brightened; an eager, greedy look filled her eyes. She actually trembled in her anxiety to secure this prize of prizes.

Maggie Oliphant, who was standing with a listless, indifferent attitude near the door, not taking the smallest part in the active proceedings that were going forward, was for the first time aroused to interest by the expression on Rosalind's face. She moved a step or two into the crowd, and when one or two timid bids were heard for the coveted treasure, she raised her own voice and for the first time appeared eager to secure something for herself.

Rose bid against her, an angry flush filling her blue eyes as she did so. Maggie nonchalantly made her next bid a little higher—Rose raised hers. Soon they were the only two in the field; other girls had come to the limit of their purses and withdrew.

Rosalind's face grew very white. Could she have knocked Maggie Oliphant down with a blow, she would have done so at that moment. Maggie calmly and quietly continued her bids, raising them gradually higher and higher. Five, six, seven, eight, nine, ten pounds: Rose had come to the end of her resources. She stepped away, and the sealskin jacket was Maggie Oliphant's property for ten guineas.

Maggie laid it carelessly on a table near, and, returning once more to her position near the door, watched the sale proceed. One by one Polly Singleton parted with her dresses, her pictures, her furniture. At last, opening a case, she proceeded to dispose of some trinkets, none of which, with the exception of the pink coral set, was of very high value. The coral set, which consisted of necklace, bracelets, earrings, and some pretty pins for the hair, was most eagerly coveted by many. Several girls bid for the coral, and Maggie, who had not raised her voice since she secured the sealskin jacket, once more noticed the greedy glitter in Rosalind's eyes.

"I can't help it," she said, turning and speaking in a low voice to Priscilla, who stood by her side. "I can't help it, Prissie. I don't want that coral a bit—I dislike it as an ornament. But something inside of me says Rosalind Merton shall not wear it. Stay here, Prissie, I'll be back in a minute."

Maggie moved forward; she was so tall that her head could be seen above those of most of the other girls.

The bids for the coral had now risen to three pounds ten. Maggie at one bound raised them ten shillings. Rose bid against her, and for a short time one or two other girls raised their previous offers. The price for the coral rose and rose. Soon Rosalind and Maggie were once more alone in the field, and now any onlooker could perceive that it was not the desire to obtain the pretty ornaments but the wish for victory that animated both girls.

When the bids rose above ten guineas, Rosalind's face assumed a ghastly hue, but she was now far too angry with Maggie to pause or consider the fact that she was offering more money for the pink coral than she possessed in the world. The bids still went higher and higher. No sound was heard but the eager voices of the two who were cruelly fighting each other and the astonished tones of the young auctioneer. Twelve, thirteen, fourteen pounds were reached. Maggie's bid was fourteen pounds.

"Guineas!" screamed Rose with a weak sort of gasp.

Maggie turned and looked at her, then walked slowly back to her place by Priscilla's side.

The coral belonged to Rose Merton, and she had four guineas too little to pay for it.

❖XVIII❖

A Black Self
and a White Self

t is quite true, Maggie," said Nancy Banister. "It *is* about the auction. What possessed you to go?"

Maggie Oliphant was standing in the center of her own room with an open letter in her hand. Nancy was reading it over her shoulder:

KATHARINE HALL,
Dec. 2.

"Miss Eccleston and Miss Heath request Miss Oliphant and Miss Peel to present themselves in Miss Eccleston's private sitting room this evening at seven o'clock."

"That is all," said Maggie. "It sounds as solemn and unfriendly as if one were about to be tried for some capital offense."

"It's the auction, of course," repeated Nancy. "Those girls thought they had kept it so quiet, but someone must have 'peached,' I suppose, to curry favor. Whatever made you go, Maggie? You know you have never mixed yourself up with that Day, Merton, and Marsh set. As to that poor Polly Singleton, there's no harm in her, but she's a perfect madcap. What could have possessed you to go?"

"My evil genius," repeated Maggie in a gloomy tone. "You don't suppose I *wished* to be there. But that horrid little Merton girl said something taunting, and then I forgot myself. Oh, dear, Nancy! What shall I ever do with that other self of mine? It will ruin me in the end. It gets stronger every day."

"There are two selves in me," replied Maggie. "And if one even approaches the faintest semblance of angelhood, the other is black as pitch."

Maggie sat down on the sofa. Nancy suddenly knelt by her side.

"Dear Meg," she said caressingly, "you're the noblest, and the sweetest, and the most beautiful girl at St. Benet's! Why can't you live up to your true self?"

"There are two selves in me," replied Maggie. "And if one even approaches the faintest semblance of angelhood, the other is black as pitch. There, it only wastes time to talk the thing over. I'm in for the sort of scrape I hate most. See, Nancy, I bought this at the auction."

She opened her wardrobe, and taking out Polly Singleton's magnificent eighty-guinea sealskin jacket, slipped it on.

"Don't I look superb?" said Maggie. She shut the wardrobe door and surveyed herself in its long glass. Brown was Maggie Oliphant's color. It harmonized with the soft tints of her delicately rounded face, with the rich color in her hair, with the light in her eyes. It added to all these charms, softening them, giving to them a more perfect luster.

"Oh, Maggie!" said Nancy, clasping her hands, "you ought always to be dressed as you are now."

Maggie dropped her arms suddenly to her sides. The jacket, a little too large for her, slid off her shoulders and lay in a heap on the floor.

"What?" she said suddenly. "Am I never to show my true and real self? Am I always to be disguised in sham beauty and sham goodness? Oh, Nancy, Nancy! If there is a creature I hate—her name is Maggie Oliphant!"

Nancy picked up the sealskin jacket and put it back into the wardrobe.

"I am sorry you went to the auction, Maggie," she repeated, "and I'm sorry still to find you bought poor Polly Singleton's sealskin. Well, it's done now, and we have to consider how to get you out of this scrape. There's no time for you to indulge in that morbid talk of yours today, Maggie, darling. Let us consider what's best to be done."

"Nothing," retorted Maggie. "I shall simply go to Miss Heath and Miss Eccleston and tell them the truth. There's no hope whatever of getting out of the affair. I went to Polly Singleton's auction because Rosalind Merton raised the worst in me. I tried to become the possessor of the sealskin jacket because her heart was set on it. I won an eighty-guinea jacket for ten guineas. I did worse even than that—I revenged myself still further upon that spiteful little gnat, Rosalind, and raised the price of her coveted coral to such an extent that I know by her face she is pounds in debt for it.

"Now, my dear, what have you to say to me? Nothing good, I know that. Let me read Aristotle for the next hour just to calm my mind."

Maggie turned away, seated herself by her writing bureau, and tried to lose both the past and the present in her beloved Greek.

"She will do it, too," whispered Nancy as she left the room. "No one ever was made quite like Maggie. She can feel tortures and yet the next moment she can be in ecstasy. She is so tantalizing that at times you are almost brought to believe her own stories about herself. You are almost sure that she has got the black self as well as the white self. But through it all, yes, through it all, you love her. Dear Maggie!"

Nancy was walking slowly down the corridor when a door gently opened and the sweet, childish, innocent face of Rosalind peeped out.

"Nancy, is that you? Do, for heaven's sake, come in and speak to me for a moment."

"What about, Rosalind? I have only a minute or two to spare. My German lecture is to begin immediately."

"Oh, you don't know the awful trouble we've got into."

"You mean about the auction?"

"Yes—yes; so you have heard?"

"Of course I've heard. If that is all, Rosalind, I cannot wait to discuss the matter now. I am very sorry for you, of course, but as I said to Maggie, why did you do it?"

"Oh, you've been talking to Miss Oliphant? Thank goodness she'll have to answer for her sins as well as the rest of us."

"Maggie is my friend, Rosalind."

"Lucky for her that she has got one true friend!" retorted Rosalind.

"What do you mean?"

"I mean what I say. Maggie is making such a fool of herself that we are all laughing at her behind her back."

"Indeed? I fail to understand you."

"You are being made a fool of too, Nancy. Oh, I did think you'd have had more sense."

"How? Speak. Say at once what you want to say, Rosalind, and stop talking riddles."

"Fly then," retorted Rosalind, "only think twice before you give your confidence to a *certain person*. A person who makes a fine parade of poverty and so-called honesty of purpose, but who can, and who does, betray her kindest and best friend behind her back. It is my private belief we have to thank this virtuous being for getting us into the pleasant scrape we are in. I am convinced she has tried to curry favor by telling Miss Heath all about poor Polly's auction."

"You mean Priscilla Peel?" said Nancy. She forgot her German lecture now. "You have no right to say words of that kind. You have taken a dislike to Prissie, no one knows why. She is good, and you should respect her."

Rosalind laughed bitterly.

"Good? Is she? Ask Mr. Hammond. Some say she is not beautiful nor interesting. Perhaps he finds her both. Ask him."

"Rosalind, I shall tell Maggie what you say. This is not the first time you have hinted unkind things about Priscilla. It is better to sift a matter of this kind to the bottom than to hint it all over the college as you are doing. Maggie shall take it in hand."

"Let her! I shall only be too delighted! What a jolly time the saintly Priscilla will have."

"I can't stay any longer, Rosalind."

"But, Nancy, just one moment. I want to put accounts right with Polly before tonight. Mother sent me ten pounds to buy something at the auction. The coral cost fourteen guineas. I have written to mother for the balance, and it may come by any post. *Do* lend it to me until it comes! *Do*, kind Nancy!"

"I have not got so much in the world, I have not really, Rosalind. Good-bye; my lecture will have begun."

Nancy ran out of the room, and Miss Merton ruefully turned to survey her empty purse and to read again a letter that had already arrived from her mother:

MY DEAR ROSALIND:

I have not the additional money to spare you, my poor child. The ten pounds which I yielded at your first earnest request was, in reality, taken from the money that is to buy your sisters their winter dresses. I dare not encroach any further on it or your father would certainly ask me why the girls were dressed so shabbily. Fourteen guineas for coral! You know, my dear child, we cannot afford this extravagance. My advice is to return it to your friend and to ask her to let you have the ten guineas back. You might return it to me in a postal order, for I want it badly. It was one thing to struggle to let you have it in the hopes that you would secure a really valuable garment like a sealskin jacket, and another to give it to you for some rather useless ornaments.

YOUR AFFECTIONATE MOTHER

❖XIX❖

In Miss Eccleston's
Sitting Room

Miss Eccleston was a dark, heavy-looking person; she was not as attractive either in appearance or manner as Miss Heath. When Maggie entered Miss Eccleston's sitting room that evening, she found the room about half full of girls. Miss Eccleston was standing up and speaking; Miss Heath was leaning against the wall; a velvet curtain made a background which brought out her massive and grand figure in full relief. Her expression was a little perplexed, and a kind of sorrowful mirth brought smiles to her lips now and then, which she was most careful to suppress instantly.

As Maggie made her way to the front of the room, she recognized several of the girls. Rosalind Merton, Annie Day, and Lucy Marsh were all present. Prissie, too, was there—she had squeezed herself into a corner. She looked awkward, plain, and wretched. She was clasping and unclasping her hands and trying to subdue the nervous tremors that she could not conceal.

Maggie, as she walked across the room, singled Prissie out. She gave her a swift glance, a brilliant and affectionate smile, and then stood in such a position that neither Miss Eccleston nor Miss Heath could catch a glimpse of her.

Miss Eccleston, who had been speaking when Maggie entered the room, was now silent. She had a notebook in her hand and was rapidly writing something in it with a pencil. Someone gave Maggie a rather severe prod on her elbow. Polly Singleton, tall, flushed, and heavy, stood close to her side.

"You'll stand up for me, won't you, Miss Oliphant?" whispered Polly.

Maggie raised her eyes, looked at the girl who was even taller than herself, and began to reply in her usual voice.

"Silence," said Miss Eccleston. She put down her notebook. "I wish for no conversation between you at the present moment, young ladies. Good evening, Miss Oliphant; I am pleased to see you here. I shall have a few questions to ask you in a minute. Now, Miss Singleton, if you please, we will resume our conversation. You have confessed to the fact of the auction. I wish now to ascertain what your motive was."

Poor Polly stammered, reddened, and looked to right and left of her in the most bewildered and unhappy manner.

"Don't you hear me, Miss Singleton? I wish to know what your motive was in having an auction in Katharine Hall," repeated Miss Eccleston.

"Tell her the truth," whispered Maggie.

Polly, who was in a condition to catch even at a straw for support, said falteringly, "I had the auction in my room because of dad."

Miss Eccleston raised her brows. The amused smile of sorrow round Miss Heath's mouth became more marked. She came forward a few steps and stood near Miss Eccleston.

"You must explain yourself, Miss Singleton," repeated Miss Eccleston.

137

"Do tell everything," said Maggie again.

"Dad is about the only person I hate vexing," began Polly once more. "He is awfully rich, but he hates me to get into debt, and—and—there was no other way to raise money. I couldn't tell dad—I—*couldn't* keep out of debt, so I had to sell my things."

"You have made a very lame excuse, Miss Singleton," said Miss Eccleston after a pause. "You did something which was extremely irregular and improper. Your reason for doing it was even worse than the thing itself. You were in debt. The students of St. Benet's are not expected to be in debt."

"But there's no rule against it," suddenly interrupted Maggie.

"Hush! Your turn to speak will come presently. You know, Miss Singleton—all the right-minded girls in this college know—that we deal in principles, not rules. Now, please go on with your story."

Polly's broken and confused narrative continued for the next five minutes. There were some titters from the girls behind her—even Miss Heath smiled faintly. Miss Eccleston alone remained grave and displeased.

"That will do," she said at last. "You are a silly and rash girl, and your only possible defense is your desire to keep the knowledge of your extravagance from your father. Your love for him, however, has never taught you true nobility. Had you that even in the most shadowy degree, you would abstain from the things that he detests. He gives you an ample allowance. Were you a schoolgirl and I your mistress, I should punish you severely for your conduct."

Miss Eccleston paused. Polly put her handkerchief up to her eyes.

"Miss Oliphant," said Miss Eccleston, "will you please account for the fact that you, who are looked up to in this college, you who are one of our senior students, and for whom Miss Heath has a high regard, took part in the disgraceful scenes that occurred in Miss Singleton's room on Monday evening?"

"I shall certainly tell you the truth," retorted Maggie. She paused for a moment. Then, with color flooding her cheeks and her eyes looking straight before her, she began:

"I went to Miss Singleton's room knowing that I was doing wrong. I hated to go and did not take the smallest interest in the proceedings." She paused again. Her voice, which had been slightly faltering, grew a little firmer. Her eyes met Miss Heath's, which were gazing at her in sorrowful and amazed surprise. Then she continued, "I did not go alone. I took another and perfectly innocent girl with me. She is a newcomer, and this is her first term. She would naturally be led by me, and I wish therefore to exonerate her completely. Her name is Priscilla Peel. She did not buy anything, and she hated being there even more than I did, but I took her hand and absolutely forced her to come with me."

"Did you buy anything at the auction, Miss Oliphant?"

"Yes, a sealskin jacket."

"Do you mind telling me what you paid for it?"

"Ten guineas."

"Was that, in your opinion, a fair price for the jacket?"

"The jacket was worth a great deal more. The price I paid for it was much below its value."

Miss Eccleston made some further notes in her book. Then she looked up.

"Have you anything more to say, Miss Oliphant?"

"I could say more. I could make you think even worse of me than you now think, but as any further disclosures of mine would bring another girl into trouble, I would rather not speak."

"You are certainly not forced to speak. I am obliged to you for the candor with which you have treated me."

Miss Eccleston then turned to Miss Heath and said a few words to her in a low voice. Her words were not heard by the anxiously listening girls, but they seemed to displease Miss Heath, who shook her head. But Miss Eccleston held very firmly to her own opinion. After a pause of a few minutes, Miss Heath came forward and addressed the young girls who were assembled before her.

"The leading spirit of this college," she said, "is almost perfect immunity from the bondage of rules. The principals of these halls have fully trusted the students who reside in them and relied on their honor. Until now, we've had no reason to complain that the spirit of absolute trust that we have shown has been abused; but the circumstance that has just occurred has given Miss Eccleston and myself some pain."

"It has surprised us, and it has given us a blow," interrupted Miss Eccleston.

"And Miss Eccleston feels," proceeded Miss Heath, "and perhaps she is right, that the matter ought to be laid before the college authorities, who will decide what are the best steps to be taken."

"You do not agree with that view, do you, Miss Heath?" asked Maggie Oliphant suddenly.

"At first I did not. I leaned to the side of mercy. I thought you might all have learned a lesson in the distress which you have caused us, and that such an occurrence could not happen again."

"Won't Miss Eccleston adopt your views?" questioned Maggie.

"No—no," interrupted Miss Eccleston. "I cannot accept the responsibility. The college authorities must decide the matter."

"Remember," said Maggie, stepping forward a pace or two, "that we are no children. If we were at school you ought to punish us, and, of course, you would. I *hate* what I have done, and I own it frankly. But you cannot forget, Miss Eccleston, that no girl here has broken a rule when she attended the auction and bought Miss Singleton's things, and even Miss Singleton broke no rule when she went in debt."

There was a buzz of approval from the girls in the background. Miss Eccleston looked angry but perplexed. Miss Heath again turned and spoke to her. She replied in a low tone. Miss Heath said something further. At last Miss Eccleston sat down and Miss Heath came forward and addressed Maggie Oliphant.

"Your words have been scarcely respectful, Miss Oliphant," she said, "but there is a certain justice in them which my friend, Miss Eccleston, is the first to admit. She has consented, therefore, to defer her final decision for twenty-four hours."

After the meeting in Miss Eccleston's drawing room, the affair of the auction assumed enormous proportions. There was no other topic of conversation. The students took sides vigorously in the matter: the gay, giddy, and careless ones voting the auction a rare bit of fun and upholding those who had taken part in it with all their might and main. The more sober and high-minded girls, on the other hand, took Miss Heath's and Miss Eccleston's view of the matter. The principles of the college had been disregarded, the spirit of order had been broken. These girls felt that the tone of St. Benet's was lowered. Even Maggie Oliphant sank in their estimation. A few went to the length of saying that they could no longer include her in their set.

Constance Field was a girl whose opinion was always received with respect. Constance, after searching in Maggie's room and wandering in different parts of the grounds, found the truant at last, comfortably established in the library with a pile of new books and magazines.

"Well, Constance, have you anything to say?"

"Not unless you want to hear me," said Miss Field in her dignified manner.

"Oh, my dear Connie, I'm always charmed, you know that."

"Well, I thought I'd like to tell you that I admired the way you spoke last night."

"Were you present?"

"No, but some friends of mine were. They repeated the whole thing verbatim."

"Oh, you heard it secondhand. Highly colored, no doubt, and not the least like its poor original."

Maggie spoke with a kind of bitter, defiant sarcasm, and a delicate color came into Miss Field's cheeks.

"At least, I heard enough to assure me that you spoke the truth and concealed nothing," she said.

"It is the case that I spoke the truth, as far as it went; but it is not the case that I concealed nothing."

"Well, Maggie, I have come to offer you my sincere sympathy."

"Thank you," said Maggie. She leaned back in her chair, folded her hands, and a tired look came over her expressive face. "The fact is," she said suddenly, "I am sick of the whole thing. I am sorry I went; now I wish to forget it."

"How can you possibly forget it until you know Miss Heath's and Miss Eccleston's decision?"

"Frankly, Constance, I don't care what decision they come to."

"You don't care? You don't mind the college authorities knowing?"

"I don't care if every college authority in England knows. I have been humbled in the eyes of Miss Heath, whom I love;

nothing else matters. Now, Constance, do let us talk of something else."

"We'll talk about Miss Peel. I don't know her as you do, but I'm interested in her."

"Oh, pray don't. I want to keep her to myself."

"Why?"

"She suits me because she loves me without question. She is absolutely sincere; she could not say an untrue thing; she is so clever that I could not talk frivolities when I am with her; and so good, so really, simply good that she keeps at bay my bad half hours and my reckless moods."

Constance smiled. She believed part of Maggie's speech, but not the whole of it, for she knew the enthusiasm of the speaker.

"I am going to Kingsdene," said Maggie suddenly. "Prissie is coming with me. Will you come too, Constance? I wish you would."

"Thank you," said Constance. She hesitated for a moment. "It is the best thing in the world for Heath Hall," she thought, "that the girls should see me walking with Maggie today." Aloud she said, "All right, Maggie, I'll go upstairs and put on my hat and jacket and meet you and Miss Peel on the porch."

"We are going to tea at the Marshalls'," said Maggie. "You don't mind that, do you? You know them, too?"

"Know them? I should think so. Isn't old Mrs. Marshall a picture? And Helen is one of my best friends."

"You shall make Helen happy this afternoon, dear Constance."

Maggie ran gaily out of the room as she spoke, and a few minutes later the three girls, in excellent spirits, started for Kingsdene.

As they entered the town, they saw Rosalind Merton coming to meet them. There was nothing in this, for Rosalind was a gay young person and had many friends in Kingsdene. Few days passed that did not see her in the old town on her way to visit this friend or that.

On this occasion, however, Rosalind was walking demurely down the High Street, daintily dressed and charming to look at, in Geoffrey Hammond's company. Rosalind was talking eagerly and earnestly, and Hammond, who was very tall, was bending down to catch her words when the other three girls came briskly round a corner and in full view of the pair.

"Oh!" exclaimed Priscilla aloud in her abrupt, startled way. Her face became suffused with a flood of the deepest crimson, and Maggie, who felt a little annoyed at seeing Hammond in Rosalind's company, could not help noticing Priscilla's almost uncontrollable agitation.

Rosalind blushed too, but prettily, when she saw the other three girls come up.

"I will say good-bye now, Mr. Hammond," she said, "for I must get back to St. Benet's in good time tonight."

She held out her hand, which the young man took and shook cordially.

"I am extremely obliged to you," he said.

Maggie was near enough to hear his words. Rosalind tripped past her three fellow students with an airy little nod and the faint beginning of a mocking curtsy.

Hammond came up to the three girls and joined them at once.

"Are you going to the Marshalls'?" he said to Maggie.

"Yes."

"So am I. What a lucky turn."

He said another word or two, and then the four turned to walk down the High Street. Maggie walked on in front with Constance. Hammond fell to Priscilla's share.

"I am delighted to see you again," she said in her eager, agitated, abrupt way.

"Are you?" he replied with some astonishment. Then he hastened to say something polite. "I forgot, we had not ended our discussion. You almost convinced me with regard to the superior merits of the *Odyssey*, but not quite. Shall we renew the subject now?"

"I had no idea until I knew Maggie that a person could have faults and yet be noble. It's a new sort of experience to me."

"No, please don't. That's not why I'm glad to see you. It's for something quite, quite different. I want to say something to you, and it's most important. Can't we just keep back a little from the others? I don't want Maggie to hear."

Now why were Miss Oliphant's ears so sharp that afternoon? Why, even in the midst of her gay chatter with Constance, did she hear every word of Priscilla's queer, garbled speech? And why did astonishment and even anger steal into her heart?

What she did, however, was to gratify Prissie immensely by hurrying on with her companion, so that she and Hammond were left comfortably in the background.

"I don't quite know what you mean," he said stiffly. "What can you possibly have of importance to say to me?"

"I don't want Maggie to hear," repeated Prissie in her earnest voice. She knew far too little of the world to be in the least alarmed at Hammond's stately tones.

"What I want to say is about Maggie, and yet it isn't."

"About Miss Oliphant?"

"Oh, yes, but she's Maggie to me. She's the dearest, the best—there's no one like her, no one. I didn't understand her at first, but now I know how noble she is. I had no idea until I knew Maggie that a person could have faults and yet be noble. It's a new sort of experience for me."

Prissie's eyes were shining now. Hammond saw the lovely expression in the eyes, and said to himself, "Good heavens, could I ever have regarded that dear child as plain?" Aloud he said in a softened voice, "I'm awfully obliged to you for saying these sorts of things of Miss—Miss Oliphant, but you must know, at least you must guess, that I—I have thought them for myself long, long ago."

"Yes, of course, I know that. But have you much faith? Do you keep to what you believe?"

"This is a most extraordinary girl!" murmured Hammond. Then he said aloud, "I fail to understand you."

They had now nearly reached the Marshalls' door. The other two were waiting for them.

"It's this," said Prissie, clasping her hands hard and speaking in her most emphatic and distressful way. "There are unkind things being said of Maggie, and there's one girl who is horrid to her—horrid! I want you not to believe a word that girl says."

"What girl do you mean?"

"You were walking with her just now."

"Really, Miss Peel, you are the most extraordinary—"

But Maggie Oliphant's clear, sweet voice interrupted them.

"Had we not better come into the house?" she said. "The door has been open for quite half a minute."

Prissie rushed in first, Miss Field hastened after, and Hammond and Maggie brought up the rear.

§XX§

A Painter

he Marshalls were always at home to their friends on Friday afternoons, and there were already several guests in the beautiful, quaint old drawing room when the quartet entered. Mrs. Marshall, her white hair looking lovely under her soft lace cap, came forward to meet her visitors. Her kind eyes looked with appreciation and welcome at one and all. Prissie received a pleasant word of greeting, which seemed in some wonderful way to steady her nerves. Hammond and Maggie were received as special and very dear friends, and Helen Marshall, the old lady's pretty grand-daughter, rushed forward to embrace her particular friend, Constance Field.

Maggie felt sore; she scarcely knew why. Her voice was bright, her eyes shining, her cheeks radiant in their rich and lovely bloom. But there was a quality in her voice that Hammond recognized—a certain ring that meant defiance and which prophesied to those who knew her well that one of her bad half hours was not very far off.

147

Maggie seated herself near a girl who was a comparative stranger and began to talk. Hammond drew near and made a third in the conversation. Maggie talked in the brilliant, somewhat reckless fashion which she occasionally adopted. Hammond listened, now and then uttered a short sentence, now and then was silent with disapproval in his eyes.

Maggie read their expression like a book.

"He shall be angry with me," she said to herself. Her words became a little wilder. The sentiments she uttered were the reverse of those Hammond held.

Soon a few old friends came up. They were jolly, good-humored girls who were all prepared to look up to Maggie Oliphant and to worship her beauty and cleverness if she would allow them. Maggie welcomed the girls and seemed to proceed to try to disenchant them.

Some garbled accounts of the auction at St. Benet's had reached them, and they were anxious to get a full report from Miss Oliphant. Did she not think it a scandalous sort of thing to have occurred?

"Not at all," answered Maggie in her sweetest tones. "It was capital fun, I assure you."

"Were you really there?" asked Miss Duncan, the eldest of the girls. "We heard it, of course, but could scarcely believe it possible."

"Of course I was there," replied Maggie. "Whenever there is something really amusing going on, I am always in the thick of it."

"Well?" Emily Duncan looked at her sister Susan. Susan raised her brows. Hammond took a photograph from a table which stood near and pretended to examine it.

"Shall I tell you about the auction?" asked Maggie.

"Oh, please, if you would be so kind. I suppose, as you were present, such a thing could not really lower the standard of the college?" These words came from Susan Duncan, who looked at Hammond as she spoke. She was his cousin and very fond of him.

"Please tell us about the auction," he said, looking full at Maggie.

"I will," she replied, answering his gaze with a flash of repressed irritation. "The auction was splendid fun! One of our girls was in debt, and she had to sell her things. I wish you could have seen her acting as her own auctioneer. Some of us were greedy and wanted her best things. I was one of those. She sold a sealskin jacket, an expensive one, quite new. There is a legend in the college that eighty guineas were expended on it. Well, I bid for the sealskin and it was knocked down to me for ten."

Maggie was clothed now in velvet and sable; nothing could be richer than her attire; nothing more mocking than her words.

"You were fortunate," said Susan Duncan. "You got your sealskin at a great bargain. Didn't she, Geoffrey?"

"I don't think so," replied Hammond.

"Why not? Oh, do tell us why not," cried the sisters eagerly.

He bowed to them, laughed as lightly as Maggie would have done, and said in a careless tone, "My reasons are complex and too many to mention. I will only say now that what is objectionable to possess can never be a bargain to obtain. In my opinion, sealskin jackets are detestable."

"What are you doing all by yourself?" he said cheerfully. "Are you always to be left like a poor little forsaken mouse in the background?"

With these words he strode across the room and seated himself with a sigh of relief by Priscilla's side.

"What are you doing all by yourself?" he said cheerfully. "Is no one attending to you? Are you always to be left like a poor little forsaken mouse in the background?"

"I am not at all lonely," said Prissie.

"I thought you hated to be alone."

"I did, the other day, in that drawing room. But these people are all kind."

"You are right. Our hostess is most genial and sympathetic."

"And the guests are nice, too," said Prissie.

"Aye, but you must not be taken in by appearance. Some of them only look nice."

"Do you mean—" began Prissie in her abrupt, anxious voice.

Hammond took alarm. He remembered her peculiar outspokenness.

"I don't mean anything," he said hastily. "By the way, are you fond of pictures?"

"I have scarcely ever seen any."

"That does not matter. I know by your face that you can appreciate some pictures."

"But, really, I know nothing of art."

"Never mind. If the painter who paints knows *you*—"

"The painter knows me? I have never seen an artist in my life."

"Nevertheless, there are some artists in the world who have conceived of characters like yours. There are some good pictures in this house. Shall I show you one or two?"

Prissie sprang to her feet.

"You are most kind," she said. "I really don't know how to thank you."

"You need not thank me at all; or, at any rate, not in such a loud voice, not so impressively. Our neighbors will think I have bestowed half a kingdom upon you."

Prissie blushed and looked down.

"Don't be shocked with me," said Hammond. "I can read your grateful heart. Come this way."

They passed Maggie Oliphant and her two or three remaining satellites. Prissie looked at her with longing and tripped awkwardly against her chair. Hammond walked past Maggie as if she did not exist to him. Maggie nodded affectionately to Priscilla and followed the back of Hammond's head and shoulders with an amused smile.

Hammond opened the outer drawing room door.

"Where are we going?" asked Priscilla. "Are not the pictures here?"

"Some are here, but the best are in the picture gallery—here to the left and down these steps. Now, I'm going to introduce you to a new world."

He pushed aside a heavy curtain, and Prissie found herself in a rather small room that was lighted from the roof. It contained in all about six or eight pictures, each the work of a master.

Hammond walked straight across the gallery to a picture that occupied a wall by itself at the further end. It represented a summer scene of deep repose. There was water in the foreground, and in the back tall forest trees in the fresh, rich foliage of June. Overhead was a sunset sky, its saffron and rosy tints reflected in the water below. The master who painted the picture was Corot.

Hammond motioned Priscilla to sit down opposite to it.

"There is summer," he said. "Peace, absolute repose. You have not to go to it; it comes to you."

He did not say any more, but walked away to look at another picture in a different part of the gallery.

Prissie clasped her hands; all the agitation and eagerness went out of her face. She leaned back in her chair. Her attitude became restful. Hammond did not disturb her for several moments.

"I am going to show you something different now," he said, coming up to her almost with reluctance. "There is one sort of rest, and now I will show you one higher. Here, stand so. The light falls well from this angle. Now, what do you see?"

"I don't understand it," said Prissie after a long, deep gaze.

"Never mind, you see something. Tell me what you see."

Priscilla looked again at the picture.

"I see a woman," she said at last in a slow, pained kind of voice. "I can't see her face very well, but I know by the way she lies back in that chair that she is old and dreadfully tired. Oh, yes, I know well that she is tired—see her hand stretched out there—her hand and her arm—how thin they are—how worn—and—"

"Hard-worked," interrupted Hammond. "Anyone can see by the attitude of that hand, by the starting veins and the wrinkles, that the woman has gone through a life of labor. Well, she does not occupy the whole of the picture. Look up a little higher in the picture. Observe for yourself that her toils are ended."

"Who is that other figure?" said Priscilla. "A woman too, but young and strong. How glad she looks and how kind. She is carrying a little child in her arms. Who is she? What does she mean?"

"That woman, so grand and strong, represents Death, but not under the old metaphor. She comes with renewed life—the child is the type of that—she comes as a deliverer. Death, with a new aspect and a new, grand strength in her face is saying to this woman, 'Come with me now to your rest. All the trouble and perplexity and strife is over. Come away with me and rest.' The name of that picture is 'The Deliverer.' It is the work of a painter who can preach a sermon, write a book, deliver an oration, and sing a song all through the medium of his brush.

"I won't trouble you with his name just now. You will hear plenty of him and his wonderful, great pictures by and by, if you love art as I do."

"Thank you," said Prissie simply. Some tears stole down her cheeks. She did not know she was crying; she did not attempt to wipe them away.

§XXI§

"I Detest It"

hortly after the girls got home that evening, they received letters in their rooms to inform them that Miss Heath and Miss Eccleston had come to the resolution not to report the affair of the auction to the college authorities. They would trust to the honor of the students at St. Benet's not to allow such a proceeding to occur again and would say nothing further on the matter.

Prissie carefully read the worded note, and then holding it open in her hand she rushed to Maggie's room and knocked. To her surprise, instead of the usual cheerful "Come in," Maggie said from the other side of the locked door, "I am very busy just now—I cannot see anyone."

Priscilla felt a curious sense of being chilled. She went back to her room, tried not to mind, and occupied herself looking over her beloved Greek until the dinner-gong sounded.

After dinner Priscilla again looked with anxious eyes at Maggie. Maggie did not stop, as was her custom, to say a kind word or two as she passed. She was talking to another girl and laughing gaily. Her dress was as picturesque as her face. But she

155

felt sure as Miss Oliphant brushed past her that her eyelids were slightly reddened, as if she had been weeping.

Prissie put out a timid hand and touched Maggie on the arm. She turned abruptly.

"I forgot," she said to her companion. "Please wait for me outside, Hester; I'll join you in a moment. I have just a word to say to Miss Peel. What is it, Prissie?" said Maggie then.

"Oh, for nothing much," replied Prissie, half frightened at her manner, which was sweet enough but had an intangible hardness about it. "I thought you'd be so glad about the decision Miss Heath and Miss Eccleston have come to."

"No, I am not particularly glad. I can't stay now to talk it over, however; Hester Stuart wants me to practice a duet with her."

"May I come to your room later on, Maggie?"

"Not tonight, I think. I shall be very busy."

Miss Oliphant nodded brightly and disappeared out of the dining hall.

Two girls were standing not far off. "The spell is beginning to work," whispered one to the other. "When the knight proves unfaithful, the most gracious lady must suffer resentment."

Priscilla did not hear these words. She went slowly upstairs and back to her own room, where she wrote letters home, made copious notes from her last lectures, and tried not to think of the little cloud that seemed to have come between her and Maggie.

Later, on that same evening, Polly Singleton was startled at hearing a low knock at her door. She opened it at once. Miss Oliphant stood outside.

"May I come in?" she asked.

"Why, of course. I'm delighted to see you. How kind of you to come. Where will you sit? I'm afraid you won't find things very comfortable, for most of my furniture is gone. But there's the bed; do you mind sitting on the bed?"

"If I want to sit at all, the bed is as snug a place as any," replied Maggie. "But I'm not going to stay, for it is very late. See, I have brought you this back."

"Listen, Miss Singleton," said Maggie. "If I keep that jacket I shall never wear it. I detest sealskin jackets. It won't be the least scrap of use to me."

Polly looked, and for the first time observed that her own sealskin jacket hung on Maggie's arm.

"What do you mean?" she said. "My sealskin jacket! Oh, my beauty! But it isn't mine, it's yours now. Why do you worry me—showing it to me again?"

"I don't want to worry you, Miss Singleton. I mean what I say. I have brought your jacket back."

"But it is yours—you bought it."

"I gave a nominal price for it, but that doesn't make it mine. Anyhow, I have no use for it. Please take it back again."

Poor Polly blushed very red all over her face.

"I wish I could," she said. "If there has been anything I regretted in the auction, besides getting all you girls into a mess, it has been my sealskin jacket. Dad is almost certain to ask me about it, for he never gave me such a handsome present before. Poor dad! He was so proud the night he brought it home."

"Well, he can be as proud as punch of you again. Here is the jacket for your very own once more. Good night."

She walked to the door, but Miss Singleton ran after her.

"I can't take it back," she said. "I'm not as mean as all that comes to. It's yours now; you got it as fair as possible."

"Listen, Miss Singleton," said Maggie. "If I keep that jacket, I shall never wear it. I detest sealskin jackets. It won't be the least scrap of use to me."

"You detest sealskin jackets? How can you? Oh, the lovely things they are. Let me stroke the beauty down."

"Stroke your beauty and pet it as much as you like, only let me say 'Good night' now."

"But please Miss Oliphant, please, I'd do anything in the world to get the jacket back, of course. But I've ten guineas of yours, and honestly I can't pay them back."

"Allow me to lend them to you until next term. You can return me the money then, can you not?"

Polly's face became on the instant a show of shining eyes, gleaming white teeth, and glowing cheeks.

"Of course I could pay you back, you—*darling*," she said with enthusiasm.

"Good night, Miss Singleton." Maggie tossed the jacket on Polly's bed, touched her hand lightly with one of her own, and left the room.

During the few days which now remained before the end of the term no one quite knew what was wrong with Miss Oliphant. She worked hard in preparation for her lectures, and when seen in public was always very merry. But there was a certain hardness about her mirth that her best friends detected and which caused Nancy Banister a good deal of puzzled pain.

Priscilla was treated very kindly by Maggie; she still helped her willingly with her Greek and even invited her into her room once or twice. But all the little half beginnings of confidence which used to burst from Maggie's lips, the allusions to old times, to deep thoughts and high aspirations, all these, which made the essence of true friendship, vanished out of her conversation.

Priscilla said to herself over and over that there was really no difference—that Miss Oliphant was still as kind to her, as valued a friend as ever—but in her heart she knew that this was not the case.

Maggie startled all her friends by making one request. Might they postpone the acting of *The Princess* until the middle of the following term?

"I cannot do it justice now," she said. "I cannot throw my heart and soul into my part. If you act the play now, you must allow me to withdraw."

The other girls, Constance Field in particular, were astonished. They even felt resentful. All arrangements had been made for this special play. Maggie was to be the Princess, and no one could possibly take her place. It was most unreasonable of her to withdraw now.

But it was one of the facts well known at St. Benet's that, fascinating as Miss Oliphant was, she was also unreasonable. In short, when Maggie "took the bit between her teeth," to employ an old metaphor, she could neither be led nor driven. After a great deal of heated discussion and indignant words, she had her will. The play was deferred till the following term, and one or two slight comedies which had been acted before were revived in a hurry to take its place.

XXII

A Black Satin Jacket

ery active preparations were being made in a certain rather humble little cottage in the country for the heroine's return. Three small girls were making themselves busy with holly, ivy, and badly-cut paper flowers to render the home gay and festive in its greeting. A little, worn old woman lay on a sofa and superintended these active measures.

"How soon will she be here now?" said Hattie. "I hope she won't talk in Latin."

"Oh, it *is* nice to think of seeing Prissie so soon," murmured Katie in an ecstasy.

"I wonder," whispered Rose, "how soon Prissie will begin to earn money? We want money even more than when she went away. Aunt Ruby isn't as well as she was then, and since the cows were sold—"

"Hush!" said Hattie. "You know we promised we wouldn't tell Prissie about the cows."

Just then a distant sound of wheels was heard. The little girls began to jump and shout; a moment later Priscilla stood in the midst of her family. A great excitement followed her arrival.

There were kisses and hugs and wild, rapturous words from the affectionate little sisters. Aunt Ruby put her arms round Priscilla and gave her a solemn sort of kiss, then the whole party adjourned into the supper room.

The feast which was spread was so dainty and abundant that Katie asked in a puzzled sort of way if Aunt Ruby considered Prissie like the Prodigal Son.

"What fancies you have, child!" said Aunt Ruby. "The Prodigal Son, indeed! Thank heaven, I've never had to do with that sort! As to Priscilla here, she's as steady as Old Time. Well, child, and are you getting up your learning very fast?"

"Pretty well, Aunt Ruby."

"And you like your grand college and all those fine young-lady friends of yours?"

"I haven't any fine young-lady friends."

"H'm! I dare say they are like other girls; a little bit of learning and a great deal of dress, eh?"

Priscilla colored.

"There are all sorts of girls at St. Benet's," she said after a pause. "Some are real students, earnestly devoted to their work."

"Have you earned any money yet, Prissie?" exclaimed Hattie. "For if you have, I do want—look—" She thrust a small foot, encased in a broken shoe, prominently into view.

"Hattie, go to bed this minute!" exclaimed Aunt Ruby. "Go up to your room, all three of you little girls! No more words— off at once, all of you. Prissie, you and I will go into the drawing room, and I'll lie on the sofa while you tell me a little of your college life."

"Aunt Ruby always lies on the sofa in the evenings now," burst from Hattie.

Aunt Ruby rushed after the plump little girl and pushed her out of the room.

"To bed, all of you!" she exclaimed. "To bed and to sleep! Now, Prissie, you are not to mind a word that child says. Come into the drawing room and let us have a few words quietly. O, yes, I'll lie on the sofa, my dear, if you wish it. But Hattie is wrong; I don't do it every night. I suffer no pain either, Prissie. Many a woman of my age is racked with rheumatics."

The last words were said with a little gasp. The elder woman lay back on the sofa with a sigh of relief. She turned her face so that the light from the lamp should not reveal the deathly tired lines round it.

Aunt Ruby was dressed in a rough homespun garment. Her feet were clad in unbleached cotton stockings, also made at home; her little, iron-gray curls lay flat at each side of her hollow cheeks.

Priscilla had seen elegance and beauty since she went away; she had entered into the life of the cultivated, the intellectually great. In spite of her deep affection for Aunt Ruby, she came back to the ugliness and the sordid surroundings of home with a pang which she hated herself for feeling. She forgot Aunt Ruby's sufferings for a moment. She longed to shower riches, refinement, and beauty upon her.

"How has your dress worn, Prissie?" said the elder woman after a pause. "My sakes, child, you have got your best brown cashmere on! A beautiful fine bit of cashmere it was, too. I bought it out of the money I got for the lambs' wool."

Aunt Ruby stretched out her hand, and, taking up a fold of the cashmere, she rubbed it softly between her finger and thumb.

"It's as fine as velvet," she said, "and I put strong work into it, too. It isn't a bit worn, is it, Prissie?"

"No, Aunt Ruby, except just round the tail. I got it very wet one day and the color went a trifle, but nothing to signify."

A vivid picture rose up before Priscilla's eyes as she thought of Mrs. Elliot-Smith's drawing room, and the dainty, disdainful ladies in their gay attire, and her own poor, little forlorn figure in her muddy cashmere dress—the same dress Aunt Ruby considered soft and beautiful as velvet.

"Oh, Aunt Ruby," she said with sudden impulse, "a great many things have happened to me since I went away. On the whole, I have had a very good time."

Aunt Ruby opened her mouth to emit a prodigious yawn.

"I don't know how it is," she said, "but I'm a bit drowsy to-night. I suppose it's the weather. The day was quite a muggy one. I'll hear your news another time, Priscilla; but don't you be turned with the vanities of the world, child. Life's but a passing day. You'll have to make up your mind to wear the cashmere for best again next term, Prissie, for, though I'm not pinched in any way, I'm not overflush either, my love."

Priscilla, who had been sitting in a low chair near her aunt, now rose to her feet.

"Ought we not to come to bed?" she said. "Come upstairs, do, and let me help you to take your things off and put you into bed. Come, Aunt Ruby, it will be like old times to help you, you know."

The girl knelt by the old woman, took one of her withered hands, then raised it suddenly to her lips and kissed it. Aunt Ruby rose slowly and feebly from the sofa.

"You may help me to get into bed if you like," she said. "The muggy day has made me wonderfully drowsy, and I'll be glad to lie down. It's only that. I'll be as pert as a cricket in the morning."

The old woman leaned on the girl's strong, young arm and stumbled a bit as she went up the narrow stairs.

When they entered the tiny bedroom, Aunt Ruby spoke again. "Your dress will do, but I have been fretting about your winter jacket, Prissie. There's my best one, though—you know, the quilted satin which my mother left me. It's loose and full, and you shall have it."

"But you need it yourself to go to church in, Aunt Ruby."

"I don't often go to church lately, child. I take a power of comfort lying on the sofa, reading my Bible, and Mr. Hayes doesn't see anything contrary to Scripture in it, for I asked him. Yes, you shall have my quilted satin jacket to take back to college with you, Prissie, and then you'll be set up fine."

Priscilla made no other response, but that night before she went to sleep she saw distinctly a vision of herself. Prissie was as little vain as a girl could be, but the vision of her own figure in Aunt Ruby's black satin quilted jacket was not a particularly inspiring one. The jacket, full in the skirts, long in the shoulders, wide in the sleeves, and enormous round the neck, would scarcely bear comparison with the neat, tight-fitting garments of the other girl graduates of St. Benet's.

"Dear Aunt Ruby!" whispered the girl.

Tears lay heavily on her eyelashes as she dropped asleep, with one arm thrown protectingly round her little sister Katie.

XXIII

The Fashion
of the Day

A thick mist lay over everything. Christmas had come and gone, and Priscilla's trunk was packed once more.

The little sisters were in bed asleep and Aunt Ruby lay on the sofa. Prissie was accustomed to her face now, so she did not turn it away from the light. The white lips, the chalky gray tint under the eyes, the deep furrows round the sunken temples were all familiar to the younger Miss Peel.

She had seen once more the old sordid life. She saw Hattie in her slipshod feet and Katie and Rose in their thin winter jackets, which did not half keep out the cold. She saw and partook of the scanty meals and tried to keep warm by the wretched fires. Once more she was part and parcel of the household. The children were so accustomed to her that they forgot she was going away again.

Tonight, however, the fact was brought back to her. Katie cried when she saw the packed trunk. Hattie pouted and flopped herself about and became unmanageable. Rose put on her most discontented manner and voice, and, finding that

Prissie had earned no money during the past term, gave utterance to skeptical thoughts.

"Prissie just went away to have a good time, and she never meant to earn money, and she forgot all about us," grumbled the naughty little girl.

Hattie came up and pummeled Rose for her bad words. Katie cried afresh, and altogether the scene was most dismal.

"You're a good girl and worthy of your poor father. . . . I'm glad I took you home and did my best for you. I'll tell him about you when I get to heaven."

Now, however, it was over. The children were in the land of happy dreams. They were eating their Christmas dinner over again and looking with ecstasy at their tiny, tiny Christmas gifts and listening once more to Prissie, who had a low, sweet voice and who was singing to them the old and beloved words: "Peace and goodwill to men."

The children were happy in their dreams, and Prissie was standing by Aunt Ruby's side. The girl knelt down by the slight, old figure and, stooping, pressed a light kiss on the forehead. Light as it was, it awoke the sleeper.

"You are there still, child?" said Aunt Ruby. "I dreamt you were away."

"Would you like me to stay with you, auntie?"

"No, my dear; you help me upstairs and I'll get into bed. You ought to be in your own bed, too, Prissie. Young creatures ought never to sit up late, and you have a journey before you tomorrow."

"Yes, but would you like me not to take the journey? I am strong, and could do all the work, and you might rest not only at night, but also in the day. You might rest always, if I stayed here."

Aunt Ruby was wide awake now, and her eyes were very bright.

"Do you mean what you say, Priscilla?" she asked.

"Yes, I do. You have the first right to me. If you want me, I'll stay."

"You'll give up that outlandish Greek, and all that babel of foreign tongues, and your fine friends, and your grand college, and your hopes of being a famous woman by and by? Do you mean this, Prissie, seriously?"

"Yes, if you want me."

"And you say I have the first claim on you?"

"I do."

"Then you're wrong; I haven't the first claim on you." Aunt Ruby tumbled off the sofa and managed to stand on her trembling old legs.

"Give me your arm, child," she said. "And—and give me a kiss, Prissie. You're a good girl and worthy of your poor father. He was a bookworm, and you are another. But he was an excellent man, and you resemble him. I'm glad I took you home and did my best for you. I'll tell him about you when I get to heaven. He'll be right pleased, I know. There, help me up to bed, my dear."

Aunt Ruby did not say any more as the two scrambled up the narrow stairs in silence. When they got into the little bedroom, however, she put her arms around Priscilla's neck and gave her quite a hug.

"Thank you for offering yourself to me, my love," she said, "but I wouldn't have you on any terms whatsoever. Go and learn all you can at your fine college, Prissie. In my young life, sewing was the great thing. Now it's Latin and Greek. Don't you forget that I taught you to sew, Prissie, and always put a backstitch when you're running a seam; it keeps the stuff together wonderfully. Now go to bed."

❧XXIV❧

Two
Extremes

ave you heard the news?" said Rosalind Merton. She
skipped into Miss Day's room as she spoke.

"No. What is it, Rose?" asked that untidy person,
turning round and dropping a lot of ribbon which she was con-
verting into bows.

"Well," she said, sinking back into Miss Day's most comfortable chair, "the feud between a certain small person and a certain great person grows apace."

Miss Day's small eyes began to dance.

"You know I am interested in that subject," she said. She
flopped down on the floor by Rosalind Merton's side. "Go on,
my love," she murmured. "Describe the development of the
enmity."

"Little things show the way the wind is blowing," pursued
Rose. "I was coming along the corridor just now, and I met the
angelic and unworldly Priscilla. Her eyelids were red as if she
had been crying. She passed me without a word."

"Well?"

"That's all."

168

"Rose, you really are too provoking. I thought you had something very fine to tell."

"The feud grows," pursued Rose. "I know it by many signs. Prissie is not half so often with Maggie as she used to be. Maggie means to get out of this friendship, but she is too proud not to do it gradually. There is not a more jealous girl in this college than Maggie, but neither is there a prouder. Do you suppose that anything under the sun would allow her to show her feelings because that little upstart dared to raise her eyes to Maggie's adorable beau, Mr. Hammond?"

As she spoke, Rosalind shaded her eyes with her hand. Her face looked full of sweet and thoughtful contemplation.

"Get your charming Prissie to flirt a little bit more," said Miss Day with her harsh laugh.

"I don't know that I can. I must not carry that brilliant idea to extremities, or I shall be found out."

"Well, what are you going to do?"

"I don't know. Bide my time."

Miss Day gave a listless sort of yawn.

"Let's talk of something else," she said impatiently. "What are you going to wear at the Elliot-Smiths' party next week, Rose?"

"I have got a new white dress," said Rose in that voice of strong animation and interest which the mere mention of dress always arouses in certain people.

"Have you? What a lot of dresses you get!"

"Indeed, you are mistaken, Annie. I have the greatest difficulty in managing my wardrobe at all."

"Why is that? I thought your people were rich."

"The fact is," said Rose in her most affected manner, "that my father has had some losses lately, and mother says she must be careful. I wanted a great many things, and she said she simply could not give them. Oh, if only that spiteful Miss Oliphant had not prevented my getting the sealskin jacket, and if she had not raised the price of Polly's pink coral!"

"Don't begin that old story again, Rose. When all is said and done, you have got the lovely coral. By the way, it will come in beautifully handy for the Elliot-Smiths' party. You'll wear it, of course?"

"Oh, I don't know."

"What do you mean? Of course you'll wear it."

"I don't know. The fact is I have not paid the whole price for it yet."

"Haven't you really? You said you'd bring the money when you returned this term."

"Of course I thought I could, but I was absolutely afraid to tell mother what a lot the coral cost; and as she was so woefully short of funds, I just had to come away without the money. I never for a moment supposed I should have such ill luck."

"It is awkward. What are you going to say to Polly Singleton?"

"I don't know. I suppose you could not help me, Annie?"

"I certainly couldn't. I never have a penny to bless myself with. I don't know how I scrape along."

Rosalind sighed. Her pretty face looked absolutely careworn.

"Don't fret, Rose," said Miss Day after a pause; "whether you have paid for the coral or not, you can wear it at the Elliot-Smiths'."

"No, that's just what I can't do. The fact is Polly is turning out awfully mean. She has come back this time with apparently an unlimited supply of pocket money, and she has been doing her best to induce me to sell her the coral back again."

"Well, why don't you? I'm sure I would, rather than be worried about it."

Miss Merton's face flushed angrily.

"Nothing will induce me to give up the coral," she said. "I bought my new white dress to wear with it. I have looked forward all during the holidays to showing it to Meta Elliot-Smith. It's the sort of thing to subdue Meta, and I want to subdue her. No, nothing will induce me to part with my lovely coral now."

She had little doubt that she could pursue those pettinesses . . . and yet retain a position as a good, innocent, and fairly clever girl.

"Well, my dear, keep it, of course, and pay for it how you can. It's your own affair. You have not yet explained to me, however, why, when it is in your possession, you can't wear it with your new dress at the Elliot-Smiths' next week."

"Because that wretched Polly has been invited also, and she is quite mean enough and underbred enough to walk up to me before every one and ask me to give her back her property."

"What fun if she did!" laughed Miss Day.

Miss Merton's face changed color several times. She clenched her small hands and tried hard to keep back such a torrent of angry words as would have severed this so-called friendship once and for all, but Rose's sense of prudence was greater even now than her angry passions. Miss Day was a useful ally—a dangerous foe.

With a forced laugh, which concealed none of her real feelings, she stood up and prepared to leave the room.

"You are very witty at my expense, Annie," she said. Her lips trembled. She found herself the next moment alone in the brightly-lit corridor.

It was over a week now since the beginning of the term. Lectures were once more in full swing, and all the inmates of St. Benet's were trying, each after her kind, for the several prizes held out to them. Rosalind Merton was a fairly clever girl. She had that smart sort of cleverness which often passes for wide knowledge. Her pretty face and innocent manner, too, helped to win her golden opinions among the lecturers.

Those who knew her well soon detected her want of sincerity, but then it was Rose's endeavor to prevent many people becoming intimately acquainted with her. She had little doubt that she could pursue those pettinesses in which her soul delighted and yet retain a position as a good, innocent, and fairly clever girl before the heads of the college.

Rose generally kept her angry passions in check, but, although she had managed not to betray herself while in Miss Day's room, now as she stood alone in the brilliantly-lit corridor she simply danced with rage. At that moment she hated Annie Day—she hated Polly Singleton—she hated, perhaps most of all, Maggie Oliphant.

She walked down the corridor, her heart beating fast. Her own room was on another floor; to reach it she had to pass Miss Peel's and Miss Oliphant's rooms. As Rose was walking slowly down the corridor she saw a girl come out of Miss Oliphant's room, turn quickly in the opposite direction to the one from which she was coming, and, quickening her pace to a run, disappear from view.

Rose recognized this girl—she was Priscilla Peel. Rose hastened her own steps and peeped into Maggie's room. To her surprise, it was empty. The door had swung wide open and the girl could see into every corner. Scarcely knowing why she did it, she entered the room. Maggie's room was acknowledged to be one of the most beautiful in the college, and Rose said to herself that she was glad to have an opportunity to examine it unobserved.

She went and stood on the hearthrug and gazed around her; then she walked over to the bureau. Some Greek books were lying open here—also a pile of manuscripts, several notebooks, a few envelopes, and sheets of letter-paper. Still scarcely knowing why, Rose lifted the notepaper and looked under it. The heap of paper concealed a purse.

A sealskin purse with gold clasps. Rose snatched her hands away, flung down the notepaper as if she had been stung, and walked back again to the hearthrug. Once more the color rushed into her cheeks, once more it retreated, leaving her small, young, pretty face white as marble.

She was assailed by a frightful temptation and she was scarcely the girl to resist it long. In cold blood she might have shrunk from the siren voice, which bade her release herself from all her present troubles by theft. But at this moment, she was excited, worried, scarcely capable of calm thought. Here was her unexpected opportunity. It lay in her power now to revenge herself on Miss Oliphant, on Prissie, on Polly Singleton, and also to get out of her own difficulties.

How tempting was Maggie's purse! How rich its contents were likely to prove! Maggie was so rich and so careless that it was quite possible she might never miss the small sum that Rose meant to take. If she did, it would be absolutely impossible for her to trace the theft to Rose Merton. No, if Maggie missed her money and suspected anyone, she would be almost forced to lay the crime to the door of the girl she no longer, in her heart, cared about—Priscilla Peel.

A very rich flood of crimson covered Rose's cheeks as this consequence of her sin flashed before her vision. The opportunity was far too good to lose; by one small act she would not only free herself, but effectually destroy the friendship of Maggie and Priscilla.

Stealthily, with her cheeks burning and her eyes bright with agitation, she once more approached the bureau, took from under the pile of papers the little sealskin purse, opened it, removed a five-pound note, clasped the purse again and restored it to its hiding place, then flew on the wings of the wind from the room.

A moment or two later Priscilla came back, sat calmly down in one of Maggie's comfortable chairs, and, taking up her Greek edition of Euripides, began to read and translate with eagerness.

As Prissie read she made notes with a pencil in a small book that lay in her lap. The splendid thoughts appealed to her powerfully; her face glowed with pleasure. She lived in the noble past; she was a Greek with the old Greeks; she forgot the nineteenth century, with its smallness, its money worries—above all, she forgot her own cares.

At last in her reading she came to a difficult sentence, which, try as she would, she could not render into English to her own satisfaction. She was a very careful student and always disliked shirking difficulties. She resolved to read no further until Maggie appeared. She closed the copy of Euripides with reluctance, and, putting her hand into her pocket, took out a note she had just received to mark the place.

A moment or two later Maggie came in.

"Still here, Prissie!" she exclaimed in her somewhat indifferent but good-natured voice. "What a bookworm you are turning into!"

"I have been waiting for you to help me, if you will, Maggie," said Priscilla. "I have lost the right clue to the full sense of this passage—see! Can you give it to me?"

Maggie sat down at once, took up the book, glanced her eyes over the difficult words, and translated them with ease.

"How lovely!" said Prissie, giving herself up to a feeling of enjoyment. "Don't stop, Maggie, please!"

Miss Oliphant smiled.

"Enthusiast!" she murmured.

She translated with brilliancy to the end of the page; then, throwing the book on her knee, repeated the whole passage aloud in Greek.

The note that Prissie put in as a mark fell on the floor. She was so lost in delighted listening that she did not notice it. But when Maggie at last stopped, Priscilla saw the little note and stooped forward to pick it up. As she glanced at the hand-writing, a shadow swept over her expressive face.

"Oh! Thank you, Maggie, thank you," she exclaimed; "it is beautiful, entrancing! It made me forget everything for a short time, but I must not listen to any more. It is, indeed, most beau-tiful, but not for me."

"What do you mean, you little goose? You will soon read Euripides as well as I do. What is more, you will surpass me, Priscilla."

"Don't say that, Maggie; I can scarcely bear it when you do."

"Why do you say you can scarcely bear it? Do you love me so well that you hate to excel me? Silly child, as if I cared!"

"Maggie, I know you are really too great to be possessed by petty weaknesses. If I ever did excel you, which is most unlikely, I know you would be glad both for me and for yourself. No, it is not that."

"What worries you then?"

"Maggie, do you see this note?"

"Yes; it is from Miss Heath, is it not?"

"It is. I am to see her tonight. I am to see Miss Heath to tell her—" Prissie paused. Her face grew deadly white. "I am to see Miss Heath to tell her—oh, Maggie! I must give up my classics.

I must. It's all settled. Don't say anything. Don't tempt me to reconsider the question. It can't be reconsidered, and my mind is made up. That's the trouble, but I must go through with it. Good night, Maggie."

Prissie held out her long hand; Miss Oliphant clasped it between both her own.

"You are trembling," she said, standing up and drawing the girl toward her. "I don't want to argue the point if you so firmly forbid me. But, seeing that at one time we were very firm friends, you might give me your reasons, Priscilla."

Priscilla slowly and stiffly withdrew her hands; her lips moved. She was repeating Miss Oliphant's words under her breath, "At one time we were friends."

"Won't you speak?" said Maggie impatiently.

"Oh yes, I'll speak. You won't understand, but you had better know—" Prissie paused again. "When I went home for the Christmas recess I found Aunt Ruby worse. You don't know what my home is like, Miss Oliphant; it is small and poor. At home we are often cold and often hungry. I have three little sisters, and they want clothes and education; they want training, they want love, they want care.

"I know enough of Greek and Latin now for rudimentary teaching, and I shall be better qualified to take a good-paying situation if I devote the whole of my time while at St. Benet's to learning and perfecting myself in modern languages. It's the end of a lovely dream, of course, but there is no doubt—no doubt whatsoever—that it is right for me to do this."

Prissie stopped speaking. Maggie went up again and tried to take her hand; Prissie drew back a step or two, pretending not to see.

"It has been very kind of you to listen," she said. "Whatever we may be to each other in future, you will understand that I

176

don't give up what I love lightly. Thank you, you have helped me much. Now I must go and tell Miss Heath what I have said to you. I have had a happy reading of Euripides and have enjoyed listening to you. I meant to give myself that one last treat—now it is over. Good night."

Priscilla left the room—she did not even kiss Maggie as she generally did at parting for the night.

§XXV§

A Mysterious Episode

hen she was alone, Maggie Oliphant sat down in her favorite chair and covered her face with her hands. "It is horrible to listen to stories like that," she murmured under her breath. "Such stories get on the nerves. I shall not sleep tonight. Fancy any people calling themselves ladies wanting meat, wanting clothes, wanting warmth. Poor, brave Prissie!"

Maggie started from her chair and paced the length of her room once or twice. "I must help these people," she said. "I must help this Aunt Ruby and those three little sisters. Penywern Cottage shall no longer be without coal, food, and warmth. How shall I do this? Prissie must not know. Prissie is as proud as I am. How shall I manage this?" She clasped her hands, her brow was contracted with thought. After a long while she left her room, and, going to the other end of the long corridor, knocked at Nancy Banister's door.

Nancy was within. It did not take Maggie long to tell the tale which she had just heard from Priscilla's lips.

"That dear little Prissie!" Nancy exclaimed.

"I don't know that she is dear," said Maggie. "I don't profess quite to understand her. However, that is not the point. The poverty at Penywern Cottage is an undoubted fact. It is also a fact that Prissie is forced to give up her classical education. She shall not! She has a genius for the old tongues. Now, Nancy, help me. Use your common sense on my behalf. How am I to send money to Penywern Cottage?"

Nancy thought for several minutes.

"I have an idea," she exclaimed at last.

"What is that?"

"I believe Mr. Hammond could help us."

Maggie colored.

"How?" she asked. "Why should Geoffrey Hammond be dragged into Priscilla's affairs? What can he possibly know about Penywern Cottage and the people who live in it?"

"Only this," said Nancy. "I remember his once talking about that part of Devonshire where Prissie's home is and saying that his uncle has a parish there. Mr. Hammond's uncle is the man to help us."

Miss Oliphant was silent for a moment.

"Very well," she said. "Will you write to Mr. Hammond and ask him for his uncle's address?"

"Why should I do this, Maggie? Geoffrey Hammond is your friend. He would think it strange for me to write."

Maggie's tone grew as cold as her expressive face had suddenly become. "I can write if you think it best," she said. "But you are mistaken in supposing that Mr. Hammond is any longer a person of special interest to me."

"Oh, Maggie, Maggie, if you only would—"

"Good night, Nancy," interrupted Maggie. She kissed her friend and went back to her room. There she sat down before her bureau and prepared to write a letter. "I must not lose any time," she said to herself. "I must help these people substantially; I must do something to rescue poor Prissie from a life of drudgery.

"Fancy Prissie, with her genius, living the life of an ordinary, underpaid teacher—it is not to be thought of for a moment! Something must be done to put the whole family on a different footing. But that, of course, is for the future. From Priscilla's account they want immediate aid. I have two five-pound notes in my purse. Geoffrey shall have them and enclose them to the clergyman who is his relation and who lives near Priscilla's home."

Maggie wrote her letter rapidly. She meant it to be a purely business note. She did not intend Hammond to see even the glimpse of her warm heart under the carefully studied words. "I am sick of money," she said to him, "but to some people it is as the bread of life. Ask your friend to provide food and warmth without a moment's delay for these poor people out of the trifle I enclose. Ask him also to write directly to me, for the ten pounds I now send is only the beginning of what I mean really to do to help them."

When her letter was finished, Maggie put her hand in her pocket to take out her purse. It was not there. She searched on the table, looked under piles of books and papers, and presently found it. She unclasped the purse and opened an inner pocket for the purpose of taking out two five-pound notes which she had placed there that morning. To her astonishment and perplexity, this portion of the purse now contained only one of the notes.

Maggie felt her face turning crimson. Quick as a flash of lightning, a horrible thought assailed her—Priscilla had been alone in her room for nearly an hour, Priscilla's people were starving. Had Priscilla taken the note?

"Oh, hateful!" said Maggie to herself. "What am I coming to, to suspect the brave, the noble—I won't, I can't. Oh, how shall

I look her in the face and feel that I ever, even for a second, thought of her so dreadfully?"

Maggie searched through her purse again. "Perhaps I dreamt that I put two notes here this morning," she said to herself. "But no, it is no dream; I put two notes in, I put four sovereigns here; the sovereigns are safe—one of the notes is gone."

She thought deeply for a few moments longer, then added a postscript to her letter: "I am very sorry, but I can only send you one note for five pounds tonight. Even this, however, is better than nothing. I will give further help as soon as I hear from your friend." Maggie then folded her letter, addressed and stamped it, and took it downstairs.

When Maggie awoke she professed not to believe in her dream; but, nevertheless, she had a headache, and her heart was heavy within her.

Miss Oliphant was an heiress, but she was also an orphan. Her father and mother were mere memories to her. She had neither brothers nor sisters. She did not particularly like her guardian, who was old and worldly wise, as different as possible from the bright, enthusiastic, impulsive girl.

She lay awake for a long time that night, thinking of Penywern Cottage, of tired Aunt Ruby, of the little girls who wanted food and education and care and love. After a time she fell asleep. In her sleep all her thoughts were with Priscilla herself. She dreamt that she saw Priscilla move stealthily in her room, take up her purse with wary fingers, open it, remove a note for five pounds, and hide the purse once more under books and papers.

When Maggie awoke she professed not to believe in her dream; but, nevertheless, she had a headache, and her heart was heavy within her.

At breakfast that morning Miss Oliphant made a rather startling announcement. "I wish to say something," she remarked in her full, rich voice. "A strange thing happened to me last night. I am casting no suspicion on anyone; I don't even intend to investigate the matter. Still, I wish publicly to state a fact—a five-pound note has been taken out of my purse!"

There were no teachers present when Miss Oliphant made this startling announcement, but Nancy Banister, Rosalind Merton, Priscilla Peel, Miss Day, Miss Marsh, and several other girls were all in the room. Each of them looked at the speaker with startled and anxious inquiry. Maggie herself did not return the glances; she was lazily helping herself to some marmalade.

"How perfectly shameful!" burst at last from the lips of Miss Day. "You have lost five pounds, Miss Oliphant. You are positively certain that five pounds have been taken out of your purse. Where was your purse?" Maggie was spreading the marmalade on her bread and butter; her eyes were still fixed on her plate. "I don't wish a fuss made," she said.

"Oh, that's all very fine!" continued Miss Day, "but if five pounds are lost out of your purse, someone has taken them! Someone, therefore, whether servant or student, is a thief. I am not narrow-minded or prudish, but I confess I draw the line at thieves."

"So do I," said Maggie in an icy tone. "Still, I don't mean to make a fuss."

"But where was your purse, Maggie dear?" asked Nancy Banister. "Was it in your pocket?"

"No. I found it last night in my bureau, under some books and papers." Maggie rose from the table as she spoke. With a swift flash her brown eyes sought Priscilla's face. She had not meant to look at her, she did not want to; but a fascination she could not control obliged her to dart this one glance of inquiry.

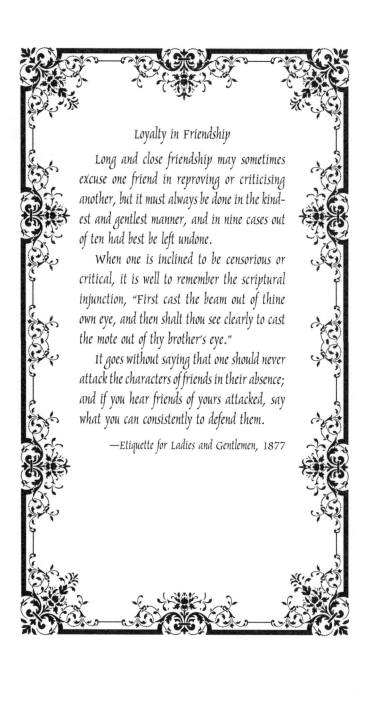

Loyalty in Friendship

Long and close friendship may sometimes excuse one friend in reproving or criticising another, but it must always be done in the kindest and gentlest manner, and in nine cases out of ten had best be left undone.

When one is inclined to be censorious or critical, it is well to remember the scriptural injunction, "First cast the beam out of thine own eye, and then shalt thou see clearly to cast the mote out of thy brother's eye."

It goes without saying that one should never attack the characters of friends in their absence; and if you hear friends of yours attacked, say what you can consistently to defend them.

—*Etiquette for Ladies and Gentlemen*, 1877

Prissie's eyes met hers. Their expression was anxious, puzzled, but there was not a trace of guilt or confusion in them. "I don't know how that money could have been taken, Maggie," she said, "for I was in your room studying my Greek." Prissie sighed when she mentioned her Greek. "I was in your room studying Greek all the evening; no one could have come to take the money."

"It is gone, however," said Maggie. She spoke with new cheerfulness. The look on Prissie's face, the tone in her voice made Maggie blush at ever having suspected her. "It is gone," she said in quite a light and cheerful way, "but I am really sorry I mentioned it. As I said just now, I don't intend to investigate the matter. I may have fallen asleep and taken the five-pound note out in a dream and torn it up or put it on the fire. Anyhow, it has vanished, and that is all I have to say. Come, Prissie, I want to hear what Miss Heath said to you last night."

"No," suddenly exclaimed Annie Day, "Miss Peel, you must not leave the room just now. You have made a statement, Miss Oliphant, which I for one do not intend to pass over without at least asking a few questions. You did not tear up that note in a dream. If it is lost, someone took it. We are St. Benet's girls, and we don't choose to have this kind of thing said to us. The thief must confess and the note must be returned."

"All right," said Maggie, "I shan't object to recovering my property. Priscilla, I shall be walking in the grounds. You can come to me when your council of war is over."

The moment Maggie left the room, Rosalind Merton made a remark. "Miss Peel is the only person who can explain the mystery," she said.

"What do you mean?" asked Priscilla.

"Why, you confess yourself that you were in Miss Oliphant's room the greater part of the evening."

"I confess it?" remarked Priscilla. "That is a curious phrase to apply to a statement. I confess nothing. I was in Maggie's room, but what of that? When people confess things," she added with a naïveté which touched one or two of the girls, "they generally have done something wrong. Now, what was there wrong in my sitting in my friend's room?"

"Oh, Miss Oliphant is 'your friend'?" said Rosalind.

"Of course, of course." But here a memory came over Priscilla; she remembered Maggie's words the night before— "You *were* my friend." For the first time her voice faltered and the crimson flush of distress covered her face. Rosalind's cruel eyes were fixed on her.

"Let me speak now," interrupted Miss Day. She gave Rosalind a piercing glance which caused her, in her turn, to color violently. "It is just this, Miss Peel," said Annie Day. "You will excuse my speaking bluntly, but you are placed in a very unpleasant position."

"I? How?" asked Prissie.

"Oh, you great baby!" burst from Rosalind again.

"Please don't speak to me in that tone, Miss Merton," said Priscilla with a new dignity which became her well. "Now, Miss Day, what have you to say?"

To Prissie's surprise, at this juncture Nancy Banister suddenly left her seat and came and stood at the back of her chair.

"I am on your side whatever happens," she remarked.

"Thank you," said Prissie.

"Now, please, Miss Day."

"You must know who took the note," said Annie Day.

"I assure you I don't. I can't imagine how it has disappeared. Not a soul came into the room while I was there. I did go away once for about three minutes to fetch my thesaurus, but I don't suppose anyone came into Miss Oliphant's room during those few minutes—there was no one about to come."

"Oh, you left the room for about three minutes?"

"Perhaps three—perhaps not so many. I had left my thesaurus in the library; I went to fetch it."

"Oh," said Rosalind, suddenly taking the words out of Miss Day's mouth, "when did you invent this little fiction?"

Prissie's eyes seemed suddenly to blaze fire. For the first time she perceived the drift of the cruel suspicion which her fellow students were seeking to cast upon her. "How wicked you are!" she said to Rosalind. "Why do you look at me like that? Miss Day, why do you smile? Why do you all smile? Oh, Nancy," added poor Prissie, springing to her feet and looking full into Nancy's troubled eyes, "what is the matter?—am I in a dream?"

"It is all very fine to be theatrical," said Miss Day. "But the fact is, Miss Peel, Miss Oliphant has lost her money. You say that you spent some time in her room; the purse was on her bureau. Miss Oliphant is rich, she is also generous. She says openly that she does not intend to investigate the matter. No doubt, if you confess your weakness and return the money, she will forgive you and not report this disgraceful proceeding to the college authorities."

While Miss Day was speaking, some heavy, panting breaths came two or three times from Priscilla's lips. Her face had turned cold and white, but her eyes blazed like living coals.

"You think," she said slowly, "you think that I stole a five-pound note from my friend; you think that I went into her room and opened her purse and took away her money; you think that of me—you! I scorn you all, I defy you, I dare you to prove your dreadful words! I am going to Miss Heath this moment. She shall protect me from this dishonor."

❦XXVI❧

In the Ante-Chapel of St. Hilda's

riscilla ran blindly down the corridor that opened into the wide entrance hall. Groups of girls were standing about. They stared as the wild-looking apparition rushed past them. Prissie was blind to their puzzled and curious glances. She wanted to see Miss Heath. She had a queer kind of instinct, rather than any distinct impression, that in Miss Heath's presence she would be protected, that Miss Heath would know what to say, would know how to dispel the cloud of disgrace which had suddenly been cast over her like a cloak.

Miss Heath's lovely private sitting room was on the ground floor. It was open now, and Prissie went in without knocking. She thought she would see Miss Heath sitting as she usually was at this hour, either reading or answering letters. She was not in the room. Priscilla felt too wild and impetuous to consider any action carefully just then. She ran up at once to the electric bell and pressed the button for quite a quarter of a minute. A maidservant came quickly to answer the summons.

She thought Miss Heath had sent for her, and stared at the excited girl.

"I want to see Miss Heath," said Priscilla. "Please ask her to come to me here. Say Miss Peel wants to see her—Priscilla Peel wants to see her, very, *very* badly, in her own sitting room at once. Ask her to come to me at once."

The presence of real tragedy always inspires respect. There was no question with regard to the genuineness of Priscilla's sorrow just then.

"I will try to find Miss Heath, miss, and ask her to come to you without delay," answered the maid. She softly withdrew, closing the door after her. Priscilla went and stood on the hearthrug. Raising her eyes for a moment, they rested on a large and beautiful platinotype of G.F. Watts' picture of "Hope."

The last time she had visited Miss Heath in that room Prissie had been taken by the kind vice-principal to look at the picture, and some of its symbolism was explained to her. "That globe on which the figure of Hope sits," Miss Heath had said, "is meant to represent the world. Hope is blindfolded in order to more effectually shut out the sights that might distract her. See the harp in her hand, observe her rapt attitude—she is listening to melody—she hears, she rejoices, and yet the harp out of which she makes music only possesses one string—all the rest are broken."

Miss Heath said nothing further, and Prissie scarcely took in the full meaning of the picture that evening. Now she looked again, and a passionate agony swept over her. "Hope has one string still left to her harp with which she can play music," murmured the young girl. "But, oh! There are times when all the strings of the harp are broken. Then Hope dies."

The room door was opened and the servant reappeared.

"I am very sorry, miss," she said, "but Miss Heath has gone out for the morning. Would you like to see anyone else?"

Priscilla gazed at the messenger in a dull sort of way. "I can't see Miss Heath?" she murmured.

"No, miss, she is out."

"Very well."

"Can I do anything for you, miss?"

"No, thank you."

The servant went away with a puzzled expression on her face.

"That plain young lady, who is so awful poor—Miss Peel, I mean—seems in a sad taking," she said by and by to her fellow servants.

Priscilla, left alone in Miss Heath's sitting room, stood still for a moment, then running upstairs to her room, she put on her hat and jacket and went out. She was expected to attend two lectures that morning and the hour for the first had almost arrived. Maggie Oliphant was coming into the house when Prissie ran past her.

"My dear!" Maggie exclaimed, shocked at the look on Priscilla's face, "Come here. I want to speak to you."

"I can't—don't stop me."

"But where are you going? Mr. Kenyon has just arrived. I am on my way to the lecture hall now."

"It doesn't matter."

"Aren't you coming?"

"No."

This last word reached Miss Oliphant from a distance. Prissie had already almost reached the gates.

Maggie stood still for a moment, half inclined to follow the excited, frantic-looking girl, but that queer inertia, which was part of her complex character, came over her. She shrugged her shoulders, the interest died out of her face. She walked slowly through the entrance hall and down one of the side corridors to the lecture room.

When the Greek lecture had come to an end, Nancy Banister came up and slipped her hand through Maggie's arm.

"What is the matter, Maggie?" she asked, "You look very white and tired."

"I have a headache," answered Maggie. "If it does not get better, I shall send for a carriage and take a drive."

"May I come with you?"

"No, dear Nancy, when I have these bad headaches it is almost necessary for me to be alone."

"Would it not be better for you to go and lie down in your room?"

"No, thank you." Maggie shuddered as she spoke. Nancy felt her friend's arm shiver as she leaned on it.

"You are really ill, darling!" she said in a tone of sympathy and fondness.

"I have not felt right for a week and am worse today, but I dare say a drive in this nice frosty air will set me up."

"I am going to Kingsdene. Shall I order a carriage for you?"

"I wish you would."

"Maggie, did you notice that Priscilla was not at her lecture?"

"She was not. I met her rushing away, I think to Kingsdene. She seemed put out about something."

"Poor little thing. No wonder—those horrid girls!"

"Oh, Nancy, if there's anything unpleasant, don't tell me just now. My head aches so dreadfully, I could scarcely hear bad news."

"You are working too hard, Maggie."

"I am not; it is the only thing left to me."

"Do you know that we are to have a rehearsal of *The Princess* tonight? If you are as ill as you look now, you can't be present."

"I will be present. Do you think I can't force myself to do what is necessary?"

"Oh, I am well acquainted with the owner of your will," answered Nancy with a laugh. "Well, good-bye, dear, I am off. You may expect the carriage to arrive in half an hour."

Meanwhile Priscilla, still blind, deaf, and dumb with misery ran rather than walked along the road that leads to Kingsdene. The day was lovely, with little faint wafts of spring in the air. The sky was pale blue and cloudless; there was a slight hoar-frost on the grass. Priscilla chose to walk on it rather than on the dusty road; it felt crisp under her tread.

She had not the least idea why she was going to Kingsdene. Her wish was to walk and walk and walk until sheer fatigue caused by long, continued motion brought to her temporary ease and forgetfulness.

Just as she was passing St. Hilda's College, she came face to face with Geoffrey Hammond. He was in his college cap and gown and was on his way to morning prayers in the chapel. Hammond had received Maggie's letter that morning, and this fact caused him to look at Priscilla with new interest. On another occasion he would have passed her with a hurried bow. Now he stopped to speak. The moment he caught sight of her face, he forgot everything else in his distress at the expression of misery that it wore.

"Where are you going, Miss Peel?" he asked. "You appear to be flying from something, or, perhaps, it is *to* something. Must you run? See, you have almost knocked me down." He chose light words on purpose, hoping to make Prissie smile.

"I am going for a walk," she said. "Please let me pass."

"I am afraid you are in trouble," he replied then, seeing that Priscilla's mood must be taken seriously.

His sympathy gave the poor girl a momentary thrill of comfort. She raised her eyes to his face and spoke huskily.

She felt as if a hand had been laid on her hot, angry heart; as if a gentle, a very gentle, touch was soothing the sorrow there.

"A dreadful thing has happened to me," she said.

The chapel bell stopped as she spoke. Groups of men, all in their caps and gowns, hurried by. Several of them looked from Hammond to Priscilla and smiled.

"I must go to chapel now," he said. "But I should like to speak to you. Can I not see you after morning prayers? Would you not come to the service? You might sit in the ante-chapel, if you did not want to come into the chapel itself. You had much better do that. Whatever your trouble is, the service at St. Hilda's ought to sustain you. Please wait for me in the ante-chapel. I shall look for you there after prayers."

He ran off just in time to take his own place in the chapel before the doors were shut and curtains drawn.

Without a moment's hesitation, Priscilla followed him. She entered the ante-chapel, sat down on a bench not far from the entrance door, and when the service began she dropped on her knees and covered her face with her hands.

The music came to her in soft waves of far-off harmony. The doors that divided the inner chapel from the outer gave it a faint sound, as if it were miles away; each note, however, was distinct. The boys' voices rose high in the air; they were angelic in their sweetness. Prissie was incapable, at that moment, of taking in the meaning of the words she heard, but the lovely sounds comforted her. The dreadful weight was partially lifted; she felt as if a hand had been laid on her hot, angry heart; as if a gentle, a very gentle, touch was soothing the sorrow there.

"I am ready now," said Hammond when the service was over. "Will you come?"

She rose without a word and went out with him into the quadrangle. They walked down the High Street.

"Are you going back to St. Benet's?" he asked.

"Oh, no—oh, no!"

"'Yes,' you mean. I will walk with you as far as the gates."

"I am not going back."

"Pardon me," said Hammond, "you *must* go back. So young a girl cannot take long walks alone. If one of your fellow students were with you, it would be different."

"I would not walk with one of them now for the world."

"Not with Miss Oliphant?"

"With her least of all."

"That is a pity," said Hammond gravely, "for no one can feel more kindly toward you."

Prissie made no response.

They walked to the end of the High Street.

"This is your way," said Hammond, "down this quiet lane. We shall get to St. Benet's in ten minutes."

"I am not going there. Good-bye, Mr. Hammond."

"Miss Peel, you must forgive my appearing to interfere with you, but it is absolutely wrong for a young girl such as you are to wander about alone in the vicinity of a large university town. Let me treat you as my sister for once and insist on accompanying you to the gates of the college."

Prissie looked up at him. "It is very good of you to take any notice of me," she said after a pause. "You won't ever again after—after you know what I have been accused of."

Just then a carriage came up and drove slowly past them. Miss Oliphant, in her velvet and sables, was seated in it. Hammond sprang forward with heightened color and an eager exclamation on his lips. She did not motion to the coachman to stop, however, but gave the young man a careless, cold bow. She did not notice Priscilla at all. The carriage quickly drove out of sight, and Hammond, after a pause, said gravely, "You must tell me your troubles, Miss Peel."

"I will," said Prissie. "Someone has stolen a five-pound note out of Miss Oliphant's purse. She missed it late at night and spoke about it at breakfast this morning. I said that I did not know how it could have been taken, for I had been studying my Greek in her room during the whole afternoon. Maggie spoke about her loss in the dining hall, and after she left the room Miss Day and Miss Merton accused me of having stolen the money." Priscilla stopped speaking abruptly. She turned her head away; a dull red suffused her face and neck.

"Well?" said Hammond.

"That is all. The girls at St. Benet's think I am a thief. They think I took my kindest friend's money. I have nothing more to say. Nothing possibly could be more dreadful to me. I shall speak to Miss Heath and ask leave to go away from the college at once."

"You certainly ought not to do that."

"What do you mean?"

"If you went from St. Benet's now, people might think that you really were guilty."

"But they think that now."

"I am quite certain that those students whose friendship is worth retaining think nothing of the sort."

"Why are you certain?" asked Prissie, a sudden ray of sunshine illuminating her whole face. "Do *you* think that I am not a thief?"

"I am as certain of that fact as I am of my own identity."

"Oh!" said the girl with a gasp. She made a sudden dart forward, and seizing Hammond's hand, squeezed it passionately between both her own.

"And Miss Oliphant does not think of you as a thief," continued Hammond.

"I don't know—I can't say."

"You have no right to be so unjust to her," he replied with fervor.

"I don't care so much for the opinion of the others now," said Prissie. "*You* believe in me." She walked erect again; her footsteps were light as if she trod on air. "You are a very good man," she said. "I would do anything for you—anything."

Hammond smiled. Her innocence, her enthusiasm, her childishness were too apparent for him to take her words for more than they were worth.

"Do you know," he said after a pause, "that I am in a certain measure entitled to help you? In the first place, Miss Oliphant takes a great interest in you."

"You are mistaken, she does not—not now."

"I am not mistaken; she takes a great interest in you. Priscilla, you must have guessed—you *have* guessed—what Maggie Oliphant is to me. I should like, therefore, to help her friend. That is one tie between us, but there is another—Mr. Hayes, your parish clergyman—"

"Oh!" said Prissie, "do you know Mr. Hayes?"

195

"I not only know him," replied Hammond, smiling, "but he is my uncle. I am going to see him this evening."

"Oh!"

"Of course, I shall tell him nothing of this, but I shall probably talk of you. Have you a message for him?"

"I can send him no message today."

They had now reached the college gates. Hammond took Priscilla's hand. "Good-bye," he said. "I believe in you and so does Miss Oliphant. If her money was stolen, the thief was certainly not the most upright and sincere girl in the college. My advice to you, Miss Peel, is to hold your head up bravely, to confront this charge by that sense of absolute innocence which you possess. In the meanwhile I have not the least doubt that the real thief will be found. Don't make a fuss; don't go about in wild despair—have faith in God." He pressed her hand and turned away.

"In the meanwhile I have not the least doubt that the real thief will be found. Don't make a fuss; don't go about in wild despair—have faith in God."

Priscilla took her usual place that day at the luncheon table. The girls who had witnessed her wild behavior in the morning watched her in perplexity and astonishment. She ate her food with appetite; her face looked serene—all the passion and agony had left it.

Rosalind Merton ventured on a sly allusion to the scene of the morning. Priscilla did not make the smallest comment. Her face remained pale, her eyes untroubled. There was a new dignity about her.

"What is up now?" said Rosalind to her friend Miss Day. "Is the little Puritan going to defy us all?"

"Oh, don't worry any more about her," said Annie, who for some reason was in a particularly bad humor. "I only wish, for my part, Miss Peel had never come to St. Benet's. I don't like anything about her. But I may as well say frankly, Rosalind, before I drop this detestable subject, that I am quite sure she never stole that five-pound note; she was as little likely to do it as you, so there!"

There came a knock at the door. Rosalind flew to open it. By so doing she hoped that Miss Day would not notice the sudden color that filled her cheeks.

§XXVII&

Beautiful
Annabel Lee

aggie Oliphant was one of the victims of fortune which, while appearing to favor her, gave her in reality the worst training that was possible for a nature such as hers. She was impulsive, generous, affectionate, but she was also perverse, and, so to speak, uncertain. She was a creature of moods, and she was almost absolutely without self-control. And yet nature had been kind to Maggie, giving her great beauty of form and face and a character that a right training would have rendered noble.

Up to the present, however, this training had scarcely come to Miss Oliphant. She was almost without relations and she was possessed of more money than she knew what to do with. She had great abilities and loved learning for the sake of learning, but till she came to St. Benet's, her governess only taught her what she chose to learn. As a child she was very fickle in this respect, working hard from morning till night one day but idling the whole of the next. When she was fifteen her guardian took her to Rome. The next two years were spent in traveling, and Maggie, who knew nothing properly, picked up

198

that kind of superficial, miscellaneous knowledge which made her conversation brilliant and added to her many charms.

"You shall be brought out early," her guardian had said to her. "You are not educated in the stereotypical fashion, but you know enough. After you are seventeen, I will get you a suitable chaperon and you shall live in London."

This scheme, however, was not carried out. For, shortly after her seventeenth birthday, Maggie Oliphant met a girl whose beauty and brilliance were equal to her own, whose nature was stronger and who had been carefully trained in heart and mind. Miss Annabel Lee was going through a course of training at St. Benet's College for Women at Kingsdene. She was an uncommon girl in every sense of the word. Her eyes were dark as night; they also possessed the depth of the tenderest, sweetest summer night, subjugating all those who came in contact with her.

Annabel Lee won Maggie's warmest affections at once, and she determined to join her friend at St. Benet's. She spoke with ineffable scorn of her London season and resolved, with that enthusiasm which was the strongest part of her nature, to become a student in reality. Under Annabel's guidance she took up the course of study that was necessary to enable her to pass her entrance examination. Miss Lee was a student in Heath Hall, and Maggie thought herself supremely happy when she was given a room next to her friend.

Those were brilliant days at the hall. Some girls resided there at this time whose names were destined to be known in the world by and by. The workers were earnest; the tone which pervaded the life at Heath Hall was distinctly high. Shallow girls there must always be where any number are to be found together, but, during Maggie Oliphant's first year, these girls had little chance of coming to the front. Maggie, who was as easily influenced as a wave is tossed by the wind, was merry with the merry, glad with the glad, studious with the studious. She was also generous, kind, and unselfish in company with those girls who observed the precepts of the higher life.

Next to Miss Lee, Maggie was one of the most popular girls in the college. Annabel Lee had the kindest of hearts, as well as the most fascinating of ways. She was an extraordinary girl; there was a great deal of the exotic about her; in many ways she was old for her years. No one ever thought or spoke of her as a prig, but the girl who could do or think meanly avoided the expression of Annabel's beautiful eyes. It was impossible for her to think badly of her fellow creatures, but meanness and sin made her sorrowful. There was not a girl in Heath Hall who would willingly give Annabel Lee sorrow.

In the days that followed, people knew that she was one of those rare and brilliant creatures who, like a lovely but too-ethereal flower, must quickly bloom into perfection and then pass away. Annabel was destined to a short life, and after her death the high tone of Heath Hall deteriorated considerably.

This girl was a born leader. When she died, no other girl in the college could take her place, and for many a long day those who had loved her were conscious of a loss of headship. In short, they were without their leader.

If Annabel in her gaiety and brightness could influence girls who were scarcely more than acquaintances, the effect of her strong personality on Maggie was supreme. Maggie often said that she never knew what love meant until she met Annabel. The two girls were inseparable; their love for each other was compared to that of Jonathan and David of the Bible story. The society of each gave the other the warmest pleasure.

Annabel and Maggie were both so beautiful in appearance, so far above the average girl in their pose, their walk, their manner, that people noticed these friends wherever they went. A young rising artist, who saw them once at St. Hilda's, begged permission to make a picture of the pair. It was done during the summer recess before Annabel died and made a sensation in the next year's Academy. Many of the visitors who went there stopped and looked at the two faces, both in the perfection of their youthful bloom and beauty. Few guessed that one even now had gone to the Home best fitted for so ardent and high a spirit.

Annabel Lee died a year before Priscilla came to the college. Whatever Maggie inwardly felt, she had got over her first grief; her smile was again as brilliant as when Annabel Lee was by her side. But the very few who could look a little way into Maggie's passionate heart knew well that something had died in her which could never live again, that her laugh was often hollow.

Maggie did not only grieve for her friend when she mourned for Annabel. She had loved her most deeply, and love alone would have caused her agony in such a loss; but Maggie's keenest and most terrible feelings were caused by an unavailing regret.

This regret was connected with Geoffrey Hammond.

He had known Annabel from her childhood. He was an old friend, and during those last, long summer holidays, which the two girls spent together under the roof of Maggie's guardian, Hammond, who was staying with relations not far away, came to see them almost daily. He was the kind of man who could win both respect and admiration. In their conversations during this lovely summer weather, these young people dreamt happy dreams together and planned a future that meant good to all mankind. Maggie, to all appearance, was heart and soul with Annabel and Geoffrey in what they thought and said.

Nothing could have been simpler or more unconventional than the intercourse between these young people. Miss Lee had known Hammond all her life; Maggie always spoke and thought of herself as second to Annabel in Geoffrey Hammond's regard. One brilliant autumn day, however, he surprised Maggie by asking her to take a long walk alone with him. No words were said during this ramble to open Maggie Oliphant's eyes to the true state of Hammond's feelings for her, but when she returned from her walk she could not help noticing Annabel Lee's unaccountable depression.

It was not until later, however, that Maggie attributed a certain pathetic, almost heart-broken, look in her friend's lovely eyes to its true cause.

Hammond was a graduate of St. Hilda's College at Kingsdene, and the three friends often talked of the happy meetings they would have during the coming winter. He was a man of large property, and the favorite amusement of these young people was in talking over the brilliant life which lay before Hammond when he took possession of his estates. He would be the ideal landlord of his age; the people who lived on his property would, when he attained his majority, enter into a millennium of bliss.

Maggie returned to St. Benet's imagining herself quite unchanged, but happiness shone out of her eyes. And there was a new, tender ring in her voice for which she could not account to herself and which added a new fascination to her beauty.

Shortly after the commencement of the term, Hammond met Miss Oliphant by accident just outside Kingsdene.

"I was going to post a letter to you," he said. His face was unusually pale, his eyes full of joy.

"You can tell me what you have written," replied Maggie in her gayest voice.

"No, I would rather you read my letter."

He thrust it into her hand and immediately, to her astonishment, left her.

As she walked home through the frosty air, she opened Hammond's letter and read its contents. It contained an earnest appeal for her love and an assurance that all the happiness of the writer's future life depended on her consenting to marry him. Would she be his wife when her three-years' term at St. Benet's came to an end?

No letter could be more manly, more simple. Its contents went straight to the depths of a heart easily swayed and full of strong affection.

"Yes, I love him," whispered the girl; "I did not know it until I read this letter, but I am sure of myself now. Yes, I love him better than anyone else in the world."

A joyous light filled Maggie's brown eyes. She rushed to Annabel's room to tell her news and to claim the sympathy that was essential to the completion of her happiness.

When Maggie entered her friend's room she saw, to her surprise, that Annabel was lying on her bed with flushed cheeks. Two hours before she had been, to all appearance, in brilliant health. Now her face burned with fever and her beautiful, dark eyes were glazed with pain.

Maggie rushed up and kissed her. "What is it, darling?" she asked. "What is wrong? You look ill; your eyes have a strange expression."

Annabel's reply was scarcely audible. Maggie was alarmed at the burning touch of her hand, but she had no experience to guide her and her own great joy to make her selfish.

"Annabel, look at me for a moment. I have wonderful news to give you."

Annabel's eyes were closed. She opened them wide at this appeal, stretched out her hand, and pushed back a tangle of bright hair from Maggie's brow.

"I love you, Maggie," she said in that voice that always had power to thrill its listeners.

Maggie kissed her friend's hand and pressed it to her own beating heart. "I met Geoffrey Hammond today," she said. "He gave me a letter; I have read it. Oh, Annabel, Annabel! I can be good now. No more bad half hours, no more struggles with myself. I can be very good now."

With some slight difficulty, Annabel Lee drew her hot hand away from Maggie's fervent clasp. Her eyes were fixed on her friend's face; the flush of fever left her cheeks; a hot flood of emotion seemed to press against her beating heart; she looked at Maggie with passionate longing.

"What is it?" she asked in a husky whisper. "Why are you so glad, Maggie? Why can you be good now?"

"Because I love Geoffrey Hammond," answered Maggie. "I love him with all my heart, all my life, all my strength, and he loves me. He has asked me to be his wife."

Maggie paused. She expected to feel Annabel's arms round her neck; she waited impatiently for this last crowning moment of bliss. Her own happiness caused her to lower her eyes. Her joy was so dazzling that for a moment she felt she must shade their brilliance even from Annabel's gaze.

Instead of the pressure of loving arms, however, there came a low cry from the lips of the sick girl. She made an effort to say something but words failed her. The next moment she was unconscious. Maggie rushed to the bell and gave an alarm, which brought Miss Heath and one or two servants to the room.

A doctor was speedily sent for, and Maggie Oliphant was banished from the room. She never saw Annabel Lee again. That night the sick girl was removed to the hospital, which was in a building apart from the halls, and two days afterward she was dead.

Typhus fever was raging at Kingsdene at this time, and Annabel Lee had taken it in its most virulent form. The doctors (and two or three were summoned) gave up all hope of saving her life from the first. Maggie also gave up hope. She accused herself of having caused her friend's death. She believed that the shock of her tidings had killed Annabel, who, already suffering from fever, had not strength to bear the agony of knowing that Hammond's love was given to Maggie.

On the night of Annabel's death, Maggie wrote to Hammond refusing his offer of marriage but giving no reason for doing so. After posting her letter, she lay down on her own sick bed and nearly died of the fever that had taken Annabel away.

All these things happened a year ago. The agitation caused by the death of one so young, beautiful, and beloved had subsided. People could talk calmly of Annabel, and although for a long time her room had remained vacant, it was now occupied by a girl who was in all respects the opposite.

Nothing would induce Maggie to enter this room, and no words would persuade her to speak of Annabel. She was merry and bright once more, and few gave her credit for secret hours of misery.

On this particular day as she lay back in her carriage, wrapped in costly furs, a great wave of misery and bitterness was sweeping over her heart. In the first agony caused by

Annabel's death, Maggie had vowed to her own heart never, under any circumstances, to consent to be Hammond's wife. In the first misery of regret it had been easy for Maggie Oliphant to make such a vow. But she knew well, as the days and months went by, that its weight was crushing her life.

If she had loved Hammond a year ago, her sufferings made her love him fifty times better now. With all her outward coldness and apparent indifference, his presence gave her the keenest pain. Her heart beat fast when she caught sight of his face; if he spoke to another, she was conscious of being overcome by a spirit of jealousy. The thought of him mingled with her waking and sleeping hours; but the sacrifice she owed to the memory of her dead friend must be made at all cost. Maggie consulted no one on this subject. Annabel's unhappy story lay buried with her, and Maggie would have died rather than reveal it.

Now, as she lay back in her carriage, the tears filled her eyes. "I am too weak for this to go on any longer," she said to herself. "I shall leave St. Benet's at the end of the present term. What is the winning of a tripos to me? What do I want with honors and distinctions? Everything is barren to me. My life has no flavor in it. I loved Annabel, and she is gone. Without meaning it, I broke Annabel's heart. Without meaning it, I caused my darling's death, and now my own heart is broken, for I love Geoffrey—I love him, and I can never, under any circumstances, be his wife.

"He misunderstands me—he thinks me cold, wicked, heartless—and I can never, never set myself right with him. Soon he will grow tired of me and give his heart to someone else, and perhaps marry someone else. When he does, I too shall die. Yes, whatever happens, I must go away from St. Benet's."

Maggie's tears always came slowly. She put up her handkerchief to wipe them away. It was little wonder that when she returned from her drive her head was no better.

"We must put off the rehearsal," said Nancy Banister. She came into Maggie's room and spoke vehemently. "I saw you at lunch, Maggie. You ate nothing—you spoke with an effort. I know your head is worse. You must lie down, and, unless you are better soon, I will ask Miss Heath to send for a doctor."

"No doctor will cure me," said Maggie. "Give me a kiss, Nance. Let me rest my head against yours for a moment. Oh, how earnestly I wish I were like you."

"Why so? What have I got? I have no beauty; I am not clever; I am neither romantically poor, like Prissie, nor romantically rich, like you. In short, the angels were not invited to my christening."

"One of two angels came, however," replied Maggie, "and they gave you an honest soul, and a warm heart, and—and happiness, Nancy. My dear, I need only look into your eyes to know that you are happy."

Nancy's blue eyes glowed with pleasure. "Yes," she said, "I don't know anything about dumps and low spirits."

"And you are unselfish, Nancy. You are never seeking your own pleasure."

"I have all I want. And now to turn to a more important subject. I will see the members of our Dramatic Society and put off the rehearsal."

"You must not! The excitement will do me good."

"For the time, perhaps," replied Nancy, shaking her wise head, "but you will be worse afterward."

"No. Now, Nancy, don't let us argue the point. If you are *truly* my friend, you will sit by me for an hour and read aloud the dullest book you can find, then perhaps I shall go to sleep."

XXVIII

"Come and Kill the Bogie"

fter reading for an hour, Nancy left her friend asleep. She went downstairs and, in reply to several anxious inquiries, pronounced that Maggie, with all the goodwill in the world, could scarcely take part in the rehearsals that night.

Maggie's appearance, therefore, with more vigor in her voice, more energy and brightness in her eyes than usual, gave at once a pleasing sense of satisfaction. She was cheered when she entered the little theater. There was a brief surprise, quickly succeeded by the comment that generally followed all her doings: "This is just like Maggie. No one can depend on how she will act for a moment."

At the rehearsal, however, if the Princess did well, the young Prince did better. Priscilla had completely dropped her role of the awkward and *gauche* girl. From the first there had been vigor and promise in her acting. Tonight there was also tenderness— a passion in her voice which arose now and then to power. She was so completely in sympathy with her part that she ceased to be Priscilla; she was the Prince who must win this wayward Princess or die.

Maggie came up to her when the rehearsals were over.

"I congratulate you," she said. "Prissie, you might do well on the stage."

Priscilla smiled. "No," she said, "for I need inspiration to forget myself."

"Well, genius would supply that."

"No, Maggie, no. The motive that seems to turn me into the Prince himself cannot come again."

Priscilla laughed joyously.

"How gay you look tonight, Prissie, and yet I am told you were miserable this morning. Have you forgotten your woes?"

"Completely."

"Why is this?"

"I suppose because I am happy and hopeful."

"Nancy tells me that you were quite in despair today. She said that some of those cruel girls insulted you."

"Yes, I got a shock."

"And you have got over it?"

"Yes. I know you don't believe badly of me. You know that I am honest and—and true."

"Yes, my dear," said Maggie with fervor, "I believe in you as I believe in myself. Now, shall we go into the library for a little?"

The moment they entered this cheerful room, which was bright with two blazing fires and numerous electric lights, Miss Day and Miss Marsh came up eagerly to Maggie.

"Well," they said, "have you made up your mind?"

"About what?" she asked, raising her eyes in a puzzled way.

"You will come with us to the Elliot-Smiths'? You know how anxious Meta is to have you."

"Thank you, but am I anxious to go to Meta?"

"Oh! You cannot be so cruel as to refuse."

After the emotion she had gone through in the morning, Maggie's heart was in that softened, half-tired state when it could be most easily influenced. She was in no mood for arguing, but she was also in so reckless a mood as to be indifferent to what anyone thought of her. The Elliot-Smiths were not in her set. She disliked them and their ways, but she had met Meta at a friend's house a week ago. Meta had been introduced to Miss Oliphant and had pressed her invitation vigorously. Miss Day and Miss Marsh were commissioned by Meta to secure Maggie at all costs.

"You will come," said Miss Day. Then coming up close to Maggie, she whispered in an eager voice, "Would not you like to find out who has taken your five-pound note? Miss Peel is your friend. Would it not gratify you to clear her?"

"Why should I clear one who can never possibly be suspected?" replied Miss Oliphant in a voice of anger. Her words were spoken aloud and so vehemently that Annie Day drew back a step or two in alarm.

"Well, but would you *like* to know who really took your money?" she reiterated, again speaking in a whisper.

Maggie was standing by one of the bookcases. She stretched up her hand to take down a volume. As she did so, her eyes rested for a moment on Priscilla.

"I would as soon suspect myself as her," she thought, "and yet last night, for a moment, even I was guilty of an unworthy thought of you, Prissie, and if I could doubt, why should I blame others? If going to the Elliot-Smiths' will establish your innocence, I will go."

"Well," said Miss Day, who was watching her face, "I am to see Meta tomorrow morning; am I to tell her to expect you?"

"Yes," replied Maggie, "but I wish to say at once, with regard to that five-pound note, that I am not interested in it. I am so careless about my money matters, that it is quite possible I may have been mistaken when I thought I put it into my purse."

"Oh! oh! But you spoke *so* confidently this morning."

"One of my impulses. I wish I had not done it."

"Having done it, however," retorted Miss Day, "it is your duty to take any steps that may be necessary to clear the college of so unpleasant and disgraceful a charge."

"You think I can do this by going to the Elliot-Smiths'?"

"Hush! You will spoil all by speaking so loud. Yes, I fully believe we shall make a discovery on Friday night."

"You don't suppose I would go to act the spy?"

"No, no, nothing of the sort—only come!"

Maggie opened her book and glanced at some of its contents before replying.

"I said I would come," answered Maggie. "Must I reiterate my assurance? Tell Miss Elliot-Smith to expect me."

Maggie read for a little in the library; then, feeling tired, she rose from her seat and crossed the large room, intending to go up at once to her own chamber. In the hall, however, she was attracted by seeing Miss Heath's door slightly open. Her heart was full of compunction for having, even for a moment, suspected Priscilla of theft. She thought she would go and speak to Miss Heath about her.

She knocked at the vice-principal's door.

"Come in," answered the kind voice, and Maggie found herself a moment later seated by the fire. The door of Miss Heath's room was shut, and Miss Heath herself stood over her.

"My dear," she said, "you look very ill. I would do anything to help you, my love," she said tenderly, and, stooping down, she kissed Maggie on her forehead.

Maggie raised her eyes.

"Perhaps another time," answered Miss Oliphant. "You are all that is good, Miss Heath, and I may as well own frankly that I am neither well nor happy, but I have not come to speak of myself just now. I want to say something about Priscilla Peel."

"But you know, Maggie, there are nobler crowns— crowns to be worn which cannot fade."

"Yes, what about her?"

"She came to you last night. I know what she came about."

"She told me she had confided in you," answered the vice-principal gravely.

"Yes. Well, I have come to say that she must not be allowed to give up her Greek and Latin."

"Why not?"

"Miss Heath, how can you say, 'why not'? Prissie is a genius; her inclination lies in that direction. It is in her power to become one of the most brilliant classical scholars of her day."

Miss Heath smiled. "Well, Maggie," she said slowly, "even supposing that is the case—she may do well to turn her attention to other subjects for the present."

"It is cruel!" said Maggie, rising and stamping her foot impatiently. "Priscilla has it in her to shed honor on our college if her present studies are not interfered with."

Miss Heath smiled at Maggie in a pitying sort of way. "I admit," she said, "that first-class honors would be a very graceful crown to encircle that young head. But you know, Maggie, there are nobler crowns—crowns to be worn which cannot fade."

"Oh!" Maggie's lips trembled. She looked down.

After a pause, she said, "Priscilla told me something of her home and her family. I suppose she has also confided in you, Miss Heath?"

"Yes, my dear."

"Well, I have come tonight to say that it is in my power to help them. I mean to put them all in such a position that Priscilla shall not need to spend her youth in drudgery. I have come to say this to you, Miss Heath, and I beg of you—yes, I beg of you—to induce my dear Prissie to go on with her classical studies. It will now be in your power to assure her that the necessity which made her obliged to give them up no longer exists."

"In short," said Miss Heath, "you will give Miss Peel of your charity and take her independence away?"

"What do you mean?"

"Put yourself in her place, Maggie. Would you take money for yourself and those dear to you from a comparative stranger?"

Maggie's face grew very red. "I think I would oblige my friend, my dear friend," she said.

"Is Prissie really your dear friend?"

"Why do you doubt me? I love her very much. Since—since Annabel died, no one has come so close to me."

"I am glad of that," replied Miss Heath. She went up to Maggie and kissed her.

"You will do what I wish?" asked the girl eagerly.

"No, my dear. It is a case in which it is absolutely impossible for me to interfere. If you can induce Priscilla to accept money from you, I shall not say a word. To tell the truth, my dear, I never admired Priscilla more than I did last night. I encouraged her to give up her classics for the present and to devote herself

"Oh, Miss Heath! You ought to do it. You ought to make her marry Mr. Hammond at once."

to modern languages and to those accomplishments which are considered more essentially feminine. As I did so I had a picture before me, in which I saw Priscilla crowned with love, the support and blessing of her three little sisters. The picture was a very bright one, Maggie."

Maggie rose from her chair. "Good night," she said.

"I am sorry to disappoint you, my love."

"I have no doubt you are right," said Maggie, "But," she added, "I have not made up my mind."

"I am very anxious about you, Maggie. Why do you speak in that reckless tone?"

"I cannot speak of myself at all tonight, Miss Heath. Thank you for what you have said, and again good night."

Maggie had scarcely left the room before Priscilla appeared.

"Are you too tired to see me tonight, Miss Heath?"

"No, my love, come in and sit down. I was sorry to miss you this morning."

"But I am glad as it turned out," replied Priscilla.

"You were in great trouble, Prissie. The servant told me how terribly upset you were."

"I was. I felt nearly mad."

"But you look very happy now."

"I am. My trouble has all vanished away. It was a great bogie. As soon as I came boldly up to it, it vanished into smoke."

"Am I to hear the name of the bogie?"

"I think I would rather not tell you—at least not now. As far as I am concerned, it cannot touch me again."

"Why have you come to see me then tonight, Priscilla?"

"I want to speak about Maggie."

"What about her? She has just been here to speak of you."

"Has she?"

"It is possible that she may make you a proposition which will affect your whole future, but I am not at liberty to say any more. Have you a proposition to make about her?"

"I have, and it will affect all Maggie's life. It will make her so good—so very, very happy. Oh, Miss Heath! You ought to do it. You ought to make her marry Mr. Hammond at once."

"My dear Priscilla!" Miss Heath's face turned crimson. "Are you alluding to Geoffrey Hammond? I know great friends of his; he is one of the cleverest men at St. Hilda's."

"Yes, and one of the best," pursued Prissie, clasping her hands and speaking in that excited way which she always did when quite carried out of herself. "You don't know how good he is, Miss Heath. I think he is one of the best of men. I would do anything in the world for him—anything."

"Where have you met him, Priscilla?"

"At the Marshalls', and once at the Elliot-Smiths', and today, when I was so miserable, at St. Hilda's, just outside the chapel. Mr. Hammond asked me to come to the service, and I went, and afterward he chased the bogie away. Oh, he is good, he is kind, and he loves Maggie with all his heart. He has loved her for a long time, I am sure, but she is never nice to him."

"Then, of course," said Miss Heath, "if Miss Oliphant does not care for Mr. Hammond, there is an end of the matter. You are a very innocent girl, Priscilla, and this is a subject in which you have no right to interfere. Far from me to say that I disapprove of marriage for our students, but, while at St. Benet's, it is certainly best for them to give their attention to other matters."

"For most of us," replied Prissie, "but not for Maggie. No one in the college thinks Maggie happy."

"That is true," replied Miss Heath thoughtfully.

"And everyone knows," pursued Prissie, "that Mr. Hammond loves her."

"Do they? I was not aware that such reports had got abroad."

"Oh, yes. All Maggie's friends know that, but they are so dreadfully stupid they cannot guess the other thing."

"What other thing?"

"That dear Maggie is breaking her heart on account of Mr. Hammond."

"Then you think she loves him?"

"I do—I know it. Oh, won't you do something to get them to marry each other?"

"My dear child, these are subjects in which neither you nor I can interfere."

"Oh! If you won't do anything, I must."

"I don't see what you can do, Priscilla. I don't know what you have a right to do. If Miss Oliphant cares for Mr. Hammond, and he cares for her, they know perfectly that they can become engaged. Miss Oliphant will be leaving St. Benet's at the end of the summer term. She is completely, in every sense of the word, her own mistress."

"Oh, no, she is not her own mistress, she is oppressed by her own bogie. I don't know the name of the bogie, or anything about it; but it is shadowing all Maggie's life; it is taking the sunshine away from her, and it is making it impossible for her to marry Mr. Hammond. They are both so fond of each other. They have both noble hearts, but the dreadful bogie spoils everything—it keeps them apart. Dear Miss Heath, I want you to come and kill the bogie."

"I must find out its name first," said Miss Heath.

XXIX

At the
Elliot-Smiths' Party

osalind Merton had been in the wildest spirits all day; she had laughed with the gayest, joined in all the games, thrown herself into every project which promised fun. Rosalind's mood might have been described as reckless. But this was not her usual condition. She was a girl who, with all her gay spirits, took life with coolness.

Today, however, something seemed wrong. She could not keep still; her voice was never quiet; her laugh was constant. Once or twice she saw Annie Day's eyes fixed upon her; she turned from their glance; a more brilliant red than usual dyed her cheeks; her laugh grew louder and more insolent.

On this evening the Elliot-Smiths would give their long-promised party. The wish of Annie Day's heart was gratified; she had angled for an invitation to this merry-making and obtained it. Lucy Marsh was also going, and several other St. Benet's girls would be present.

Early in the evening Rosalind retired to her own room, locked her door, and, taking out her new white dress, laid it across the bed. It was a very pretty dress, made of soft silk that

The Hair

There is nothing that so adds to the charm of an individual as a good head of hair. The complexion and the features may be perfect, but if the hair is thin and harsh they all pass for little. On the other hand, magnificent locks will atone for other deficiencies.

Formerly, the use of a fine-tooth comb was considered essential to the proper care of the hair, but in general, to the careful brusher, the fine comb is not necessary.

The brush should be of moderate hardness, not too hard. The hair should be separated, in order that the head itself may be well brushed. The hair should be brushed for at least twenty minutes in the morning, for ten minutes when it is dressed in the middle of the day, and for a like period at night.

Those whose hair is glossy and shiny need nothing to render it so; but when the hair is harsh, poor, and dry, nothing lubricates better than pure, unscented salad oil. But take care not to use the oil too freely. An over-oiled head of hair is vulgar and offensive.

—*Etiquette for Ladies and Gentlemen*, 1877

did not rustle but lay in graceful puffs and folds. It was just the dress to make this young, slight figure of Rosalind's look absolutely charming. She stood over it now and regarded it lovingly. The dress had been obtained, like most of Rosalind's possessions, by maneuvers. She had made up a piteous story, and her adoring mother had listened and contrived to deny herself and some of Rosalind's younger sisters in order to purchase the white robe on which the young girl's heart was set.

Deliberately and slowly Rosalind made her toilet. Her golden, curling hair was brushed out and then carefully coiled around her head. Rosalind had no trouble with her hair: a touch or two, a pin stuck here, a curl arranged there, and the arrangement became perfect—the glistening mass lay in natural waves over the small, graceful head.

When Rosalind's hair was arranged to her satisfaction, she put on her lovely white dress. She stood before her long glass, a white-robed little figure, smiles round her lips, a sweet, bright color in her cheeks, a dewy look in her baby-blue eyes. Rosalind's toilet was all but finished, but now she hesitated. Should she go to the Elliot-Smiths' as she was, or should she give the last finishing touch to render herself perfect—should she wear her beautiful coral ornaments?

The coral was now her own, paid for to the uttermost farthing; Polly Singleton could not come up to Rosalind and disgrace her in public by demanding her coral back again. Unlocking a drawer in her bureau, she took out a case. She touched the spring of the case, opened it, and looked at her coral lovingly. The necklace, the bracelets, the earrings, and pins for the hair looked beautiful on their velvet pillow. She had dreamt many times of the triumphs that would be hers when she appeared at the Elliot-Smiths' in her white silk dress, just tipped with the slight color which the pink coral ornaments would bestow. Rosalind had likened herself to all kinds of lovely things—to a daisy in the field, to a briar rose—in short, to every flower that denoted the perfection of innocence.

Yet as she held the coral necklace in her hand tonight, she hesitated deeply whether it would be wise to appear at the Elliot-Smiths' in her treasured ornaments.

Oh, yes, there was a risk—but Rosalind's vanity was greater than her fears.

Rose had not felt comfortable all day. She had tried to crush the little voice in her heart which would persistently cry, "Shame! shame! You are the meanest, the most wicked girl at St. Benet's; you have done something for which you could be put in prison."

The voice had little opportunity of making itself heard that day, and Rosalind had every hope that her sin would never be found out. Nevertheless, she could not help feeling uneasy; for why did Annie Day, her own chosen and particular friend, so persistently avoid her? Why had Lucy Marsh refused to walk with her yesterday? And why did Annie so often look at her with meaning and inquiry in her eyes? These glances of Annie's caused Rosalind's heart to beat too quickly.

She felt as she stood now before her glass that, after all, she was doing a rash thing in wearing her coral. Annie Day knew of her money difficulties; Annie knew how badly Rosalind had wanted four guineas to pay the debt she still owed for the ornaments. If Rosalind wore them tonight, Annie would ask numerous questions. Oh, yes, there was a risk—there was a decided risk—but Rosalind's vanity was greater than her fears.

There came a knock at her room door. To Rosalind's surprise, Annie Day's voice, with an extremely friendly tone in it, was heard outside.

"Are you ready, Rosie?" she cried. "If you are, there is just room for you in the fly with Lucy Marsh and Polly Singleton and myself."

"Oh, thank you!" cried Rosalind from the other side of the door. Just wait one moment, Annie, and I will be with you."

Both fear and hesitation vanished at the friendly tones of Annie's voice. She hastily fastened on her necklace and earrings, slipped on her bracelets, and stuck the coral pins in her hair. She saw a dazzling little image in the glass and turned away with a glad, proud smile.

She wrapped herself from head to foot in a long, white opera cloak, pulled the hood over her head, seized her gloves and fan, and opened the door. The coral could not be seen now, and Annie, who was also in white, took her hand and ran with her down the corridor.

A few moments later the four girls arrived at the Elliot-Smiths' and were shown into a dressing room on the ground floor to divest themselves of their wraps. They were among the earliest of the arrivals, and Annie Day had both space and opportunity to rush up to Rosalind and exclaim at the perfect combination of white silk and pink coral.

"Lucy, Lucy!" she said, "Do come and look at Rosalind's coral! Oh, poor Polly! You must miss your ornaments; but I am obliged frankly to confess, my dear, that they are more becoming to this little cherub than they ever were to you."

Polly was loudly dressed in blue silk. She came up and turned Rosalind around, and, putting her hand on her neck, lifted the necklace and looked at it affectionately.

She was also in white, but without any ornament, except a solitary diamond star which blazed in the rich coils of her hair.

"I did love those ornaments," she said. "But, of course, I can't grudge them to you, Rose. You paid a good sum for them— didn't you dear?"

"You have paid off the debt? I congratulate you, Rose," said Annie Day.

"Yes," said Rosalind, blushing.

"I am glad you were able to get the money, my dear."

"And I wish she hadn't got it," retorted Polly. "Money is of no moment to me now. Dad is just rolling in wealth, and I have, in consequence, more money than I know what to do with. I confess I never felt crosser in my life than when you brought me that five-pound note last Monday night, Miss Merton."

Rosalind colored, then grew very pale. She saw Annie Day's eyes blaze and darken. She felt that her friend was putting two and two together and drawing a conclusion in her own mind. Annie turned abruptly from Rosalind, and, touching Lucy Marsh on the arm, walked with her out of the dressing room. The unsuspecting Polly brought up the rear with Rosalind.

The four girls entered the drawing room, and Rosalind tried to forget the sick fear which was creeping round her heart in the excitement of the moment.

Nearly an hour later Maggie Oliphant arrived. She was also in white but without any ornament, except a solitary diamond star that blazed in the rich coils of her hair. The beautiful Miss Oliphant was received with enthusiasm. Maggie herself never felt less conscious of beauty, and the admiration that greeted her gave her a momentary feeling of surprise—almost of displeasure.

Meta Elliot-Smith and her mother buzzed round Maggie and expressed their gratitude to her for coming.

"We expect a friend of yours to arrive presently," said Meta. "Mr. Geoffrey Hammond. You know Mr. Hammond, don't you? I have had a note from him. He says he will look in as soon after ten as possible. I am so glad; I was dreadfully afraid he couldn't come, for he had to go suddenly into the country at the beginning of this week. You know Mr. Hammond very well, don't you, Miss Oliphant?"

"Yes," replied Maggie in her careless voice. "He is quite an old friend of mine."

"You will be glad to see him?"

"Very glad."

Meta looked at her in a puzzled way. Reports of Hammond's love affair had reached her ears. She had expected to see emotion and confusion on Maggie's face; it looked bright and pleased. Her "very glad" had a genuine ring about it.

Meta was obliged with great reluctance to leave her guest, and a moment later Annie Day came up eagerly to Maggie's side.

"It's all right," she said, drawing Miss Oliphant into the shelter of a window. "I have found out all I want to know."

"What is that?" asked Maggie.

"Rosalind Merton is the thief."

"Miss Day, how can you say such dreadful things?"

"How can Rosalind do them? I am awfully sorry—indeed, I am disgusted—but the facts are too plain." Miss Day then in a few eager whispers gave her chain of evidence. Rosalind's distress; her passionate desire to keep the coral; her entreaties that Miss Day would lend her four guineas; her assurances that she had not a penny in the world to pay her debt; her fears that it was utterly useless for her to expect the money from her mother. Then the curious fact that, on the very same evening, Polly Singleton should have been given a five-pound note by Rosalind.

"There is not the least doubt," concluded Miss Day, "that Rosalind must have gone into your room, Miss Oliphant, and stolen the note while Priscilla was absent. You know Miss Peel said that she did leave your room for a moment or two to fetch her thesaurus. Rosalind must have seized the opportunity."

Maggie's face turned white; her eyes were full of indignation and horror.

"Something must be done," continued Annie. "I am no prude, but I draw the line at thieves. Miss Merton ought to be expelled. She is not fit to speak to one of us."

"The affair is mine," said Maggie after a pause. "You must let me deal with it."

"Will you?"

"I certainly will."

"Tonight?"

"I cannot say. I must think. The whole thing is terrible; it upsets me."

"I thought you would feel it. I am a good bit upset myself, and so is Lucy Marsh."

"Does Miss Marsh know, too? In that case, Miss Day, it will, I fear, be my duty to consult Miss Heath. Oh, I must think. I can do nothing hastily. Please, Miss Day, keep your own counsel for the present, and ask Miss Marsh to do the same."

Annie Day ran off, and Maggie stood by the open window looking out at the starry night. Her head ached; her pulses beat; she felt sick and tired. She wished she had not come. A voice close by made her start—a hand not only clasped hers, but held it firmly for a moment. She looked up and said with a sudden impulse, "Oh, Geoffrey! I am glad you are here." Then, with a burning blush, she withdrew her hand from Hammond's.

"Can I help you?" he asked. Hammond's heart was beating fast; her words were tingling in his ears, but his tone was quiet.

"Can I help you?" he repeated. "Here is a seat." He pulled a chair from behind a curtain, and Maggie dropped into it.

"Something is wrong," she said. "Something dreadful has happened."

"May I know what it is?"

"I don't think I have any right to tell you. It is connected with the college; but it has given me a blow. I came here against my will, and now I don't want to talk to anyone."

"That can be easily managed. I will stand here and keep off all intruders."

"Thank you." Maggie put her hand to her forehead.

The headache, which had scarcely left her for a fortnight, was now so acute that all her thoughts were confused; she felt as if she were walking in a dream. It seemed perfectly right and natural that Hammond should stand by her side and protect her from the crowd; it seemed natural to her at that moment, natural and even right to appeal to him.

After a long pause he said, "I am afraid I also have bad news!"

"How?"

"I went to see my uncle, Mr. Hayes."

"Yes, it was good of you—I remember."

"I failed in my mission. Mr. Hayes says that Miss Ruby Peel, our Prissie's aunt, would rather die than accept help from anyone."

"Oh, how obstinate some people are!" replied Maggie wearily. "Happiness, help, and succor come to their very door and they turn these good things away."

"That is true," replied Hammond. "I am firmly convinced," he added, "that the good angel of happiness is within the reach of most of us once at least in our lives, but for a whim—often for a mere whim—we tell him to go."

Maggie's face grew very white. "I must say good-bye. I am going home," she said, rising. Then she added, looking full at Hammond, "Sometimes it is necessary to reject happiness; and necessity ought not to be spoken of as a whim."

XXX

"If I Had Known You Sooner"

s Maggie was leaving the crowded drawing room, she came face to face with Rosalind. One of those impulses which always guided her, more or less, made her stop suddenly and put her hand on the young girl's shoulder.

"Will you come home with me?" she asked.

Rosalind was talking gaily at the moment to a very young undergraduate.

"I am grateful to you," she began, "but I have arranged to return to St. Benet's with Miss Day and Miss Marsh."

"I should like you to come now with me," persisted Maggie in a grave voice.

Something in her tone caused Rosalind to turn pale. The sick fear, which had never been absent from her heart during the evening, became on the instant intolerable. She turned to the young lad with whom she had been flirting, bade him a hasty and indifferent "good night," and followed Maggie out of the room.

Hammond accompanied the two girls downstairs, got their cab for them, and helped them in.

229

After Rosalind consented to come home, Miss Oliphant did not address another word to her. Rosalind sat huddled up in a corner of the cab. Maggie kept the window open and looked out. The clear moonlight shone on her white face and glistened on her dress. Rosalind kept glancing at her. The guilty girl's terror of the silent figure by her side grew greater each moment.

The girls reached Heath Hall, and Maggie again touched Rosalind on her arm.

"Come to my room," she said. "I want to say something to you."

Without waiting for a reply she went on herself in front. Rosalind followed, shaking in every limb.

The moment Maggie closed her room door, Rosalind flung her cloak off her shoulders, and, falling on her knees, caught the hem of Maggie's dress and covered her face with it.

"Don't, Rosalind; get up," said Miss Oliphant in a tone of disgust.

"Oh, Maggie, Maggie, do be merciful! Do forgive me! Don't send me to prison, Maggie—don't!"

"Get off your knees at once, or I don't know what I shall do," replied Maggie.

Rosalind sprang to her feet. She crouched up against the door, her eyes wide open. Maggie came and faced her.

"Oh, don't!" said Miss Merton with a little shriek, "don't look at me like that!" She put up her hand to her neck and began to unfasten her coral necklace. She took it off, slipped her bracelets from her arms, took her earrings out, and removed her pins.

"You can have them all," she said, holding out the coral. "They are worth a great deal more—a great deal more than the money I—*took!*"

"Lay them down," said Maggie. "Do you think I could touch that coral? Oh, Rosalind," she added, a sudden rush of intense feeling coming into her voice, "I pity you! I pity any girl who has so base a soul."

Rosalind began to sob freely. "You don't know how I was tempted," she said. "I went through a dreadful time, and you were the cause—you know you were, Maggie. You raised the price of that coral so wickedly, I felt as if there were a fiend in me. You did not want the sealskin jacket, but you bid against me and won it. Then I felt mad, and whatever you had offered for the coral, I should have bidden higher. It was all your fault; it was you who got me into debt. I would not be in the awful, awful plight I am in tonight but for you, Maggie."

"Hush!" said Maggie. The pupils of her eyes dilated curiously.

"The fruits of my bad half hours," she murmured under her breath. After a long pause she said, "There is some truth in your words, Rosalind; I did help you to get into this false position. I am sorry; and when I tell Miss Heath the whole circumstance—as I must tomorrow—you may be sure I shall not exonerate myself!"

"Oh, Maggie, Maggie, you won't tell Miss Heath! If you do, I am certain to be expelled, and my mother—my mother will die. She is not strong just now, and this will kill her. You cannot be so cruel as to kill my mother, Maggie Oliphant, particularly when you yourself got me into this."

"I did not get you into this," retorted Maggie. "I know I am not blameless in the matter; but could I imagine for a moment that any girl, any girl who belonged to this college, could debase herself to steal and then throw the blame on another? Nancy Banister has told me, Rose, how cruelly you spoke to Priscilla—what agony your cruel words cost her.

"Now, stop crying; I have not brought you here to discuss your wickedness with you. I shall tell the whole circumstance to Miss Heath in the morning. It is my plain duty to do so, and no words of yours can prevent me."

With a stifled cry Rosalind Merton again fell on her knees.

"Get up," said Maggie. "Get up at once, or I shall bring Miss Heath here now. Your crime, Rosalind, is known to Miss Day and to Miss Marsh. Even without consulting Miss Heath, I think I can say that you had better leave St. Benet's by the first train in the morning."

"Oh, yes—yes! That would be the best thing to do."

"You are to go home, remember."

"Yes, I will certainly go home. But, Maggie, I have no money—I have literally no money."

"I will ask Priscilla Peel to go with you to the railway station, and I will give her sufficient money to pay your fare to London—you live in London, don't you?"

"Yes, at Bayswater."

"What is your address?"

"19 Queen Street, Bayswater."

"Priscilla shall telegraph to your mother when you start, and ask her to meet you at King's Cross."

Rosalind's face grew paler and paler. "What excuse am I to give to mother?" she asked.

"That is your own affair; I have no doubt you will find something to say. I should advise you, Rosalind, to tell your poor mother the truth, for she is certain to hear all about it from Miss Heath the following morning."

"Oh, what a miserable, miserable girl I am, Maggie!"

"You are a very miserable and sinful girl. But I don't want to speak of that now, Rosalind. There is something you must do before you leave."

"What is that?"

"You must go to Priscilla Peel and humbly beg her pardon."

"Oh, I cannot, I cannot! You have no idea how I hate Priscilla."

"I am not surprised; the children of darkness generally hate those who walk in the light."

"Maggie, I *can't* beg her pardon."

"I certainly shall not force you. But, unless you beg Priscilla's pardon and confess to her the wicked deed you have done, I shall lend you no money to go home. You can go to your room now, Rosalind. I am tired and wish to go to bed. You will be able to let me know your decision in the morning."

Rosalind turned slowly away. She reached her room before the other girls had arrived home, and tossing the coral ornaments on her dressing table, she flung herself across her bed and gave way to the most passionate, heartbroken sobs that had ever rent her small frame.

She was still sobbing, but more quietly for the force of her passion had exhausted her, when a very light touch on her shoulder caused her to raise herself and look up wildly. Prissie was bending over her.

"I knocked several times," she said, "but you did not hear me, so I came in. You will be sick if you cry like this, Rose. Let me help you go to bed."

"No, no. Please don't touch me. I don't want you, of all people, to do anything for me."

"I wish you would let me undress you. I have often helped Aunt Ruby to go to bed when she was very tired. Come, Rose, don't turn away from me. Why should you?"

"Priscilla, you are the last person in the world who ought to be kind to me just now. You don't know, you can never, never guess, what I did to you."

"Yes, I can partly guess, but I don't want to think of it."

"Listen, Prissie. When I stole that money, I hoped people would accuse you of the theft."

Prissie's eyes filled with tears. "It was a dreadful thing to do," she said faintly.

"Oh, I knew you could never forgive me."

"I do forgive you."

"What! Aren't you angry? Aren't you frantic with rage and passion?"

"I don't wish to think of myself at all. I want to think of you. You are the one to be pitied."

"I? Who could pity me?"

"Well, Rosalind, I do," answered Priscilla in a slow voice. "You have sunk so low, you have done such a dreadful thing, the kind of thing that the angels in heaven would grieve over."

"Oh, please don't talk to me of them."

"And then, Rosalind," continued Prissie, "you look so unlike a girl who would do this sort of thing. I have a little sister at home—a dear, little innocent sister, and her eyes are blue like yours, and she is fair, too, as you are fair. I love her, and I think all good things of her. Rosalind, I fancy that your mother thinks good things of you. I imagine that she is proud of you, and that she loves to look at your pretty face."

"Oh, don't—don't!" sobbed Rosalind. "Oh, poor mother, poor mother!" She burst into softened and sorrowful weeping. The hardness of her heart had melted for the time under the influence of Priscilla's tender words.

"I wish I had known you sooner," whispered Rose when Prissie bent down and kissed her before leaving her for the night. "Perhaps I might have been a good girl if I had really known you sooner, Priscilla Peel."

⚜XXXI⚜

A Message

Early the next morning Rosalind Merton left St. Benet's College, never to come back. She took all her possessions with her, even the pink coral, which not a girl in the college would have accepted at her hands. Annie Day and Lucy Marsh were not the sort of people to keep their secret long, and before the day of her departure had expired nearly everyone at Heath Hall knew of Rosalind's crime. Miss Heath was made acquainted with the whole story at an early hour that morning.

"I may have done very wrong to let her go without obtaining your permission, Miss Heath," said Maggie, when the story was finished. "If so, please forgive me, and also allow me to say that, were the same thing to occur again, I fear I should act in the same way. My primary object in giving Rosalind money to go home this morning was to save the college from any open slur being cast upon it."

Miss Heath's face had grown very pale while Maggie was speaking. She was quite silent for a moment or two after the

236

story was finished; then, going up to Miss Oliphant, she took her hand and kissed her.

"On the whole, my dear," she said, "I am obliged to you. Had this story been told me while Miss Merton was in the house I should have been obliged to detain her until all the facts of this disgraceful case were laid before the college authorities, and then, of course, there would have been no course open but to publicly expel her. I'll say nothing now about the rule you have broken, for, of course, you had no right to assist Rosalind to go home without permission. However, it lies within my discretion to forgive you, Maggie, so take my kiss, dear."

The vice-principal and Miss Oliphant talked for some little time longer over Rosalind's terrible fall, and, as Miss Heath felt confident that the story would get abroad in the college, she said she would be forced to mention the circumstances to their principal, Miss Vincent, and also to say something in public to the girls of Heath Hall on the subject.

"And now we will turn to something else," she said. "I am concerned at those pale cheeks, Maggie. My dear," she said, as the young girl colored brightly, "your low spirits weigh on my heart."

"Oh, don't mind me," said Maggie hastily.

"It is scarcely kind to say this to one who loves you. I have been many years vice-principal of this hall, and no girl, except Annabel Lee, has come so close to my heart as you have, Maggie. Some girls come here, spend the required three years, and go away again without making much impression on anyone. In your case this will not be so. I have not the least doubt that you will pass your honors examination with credit in the summer. You will then leave us, but not to be forgotten. I for one, Maggie, can never forget you."

"How good you are!" said Maggie.

Tears trembled in the eyes which were far too proud to weep except in private.

Miss Heath looked attentively at the young student for whom she felt so strong an interest. Priscilla's words had scarcely been absent from her night or day since they were spoken.

"Maggie ought to marry Mr. Hammond. Maggie loves him and he loves her, but a bogie stands in the way." Night and day Miss Heath had pondered these words. Now, looking at the fair face, she resolved to take the initiative in a matter which she considered quite outside her province.

"Sit down, Maggie," she said. "I think the time has come for me to tell you something which has lain as a secret on my heart for over a year."

Maggie looked up in surprise, then dropped into a chair and folded her hands in her lap. She was slightly surprised at Miss Heath's tone, but not as yet intensely interested.

"You know, my dear," she said, "that I never interfere with the life a student lives *outside* this hall. Provided she obeys the rules and mentions the names of the friends she visits, she is at liberty, practically, to do as she pleases in those hours which are not devoted to lectures. A girl at St. Benet's may have a very great friend at Kingsdene or elsewhere of whom the principals of the college know nothing. I think I may add with truth that were the girl to confide in the principal of her college in case of any friendship developing into—into love, she would receive the deepest sympathy and the tenderest counsels. The principal who was confided in would regard herself for the time being as the young girl's mother."

Maggie's eyes were lowered now, her lips trembled; she played nervously with a flower which she held in her hand.

"I must apologize," continued Miss Heath, "for having alluded to a subject which may not in the least concern you, my dear. My excuse for doing so is that what I have to tell you directly bears on the question of marriage. I would have spoken to you long ago, but, until lately, until a few days ago, I had not the faintest idea that such a subject had even distantly visited your mind."

"Who has dared to interfere—to spread rumors? I am not going to marry. I shall never marry."

"Who told you that it had?" questioned Maggie. She spoke with anger. "Who has dared to interfere—to spread rumors? I am not going to marry. I shall never marry."

"It is not in my power at present to tell you how the rumor has reached me," continued Miss Heath, "but, having reached me, I want to say a few words about—about Annabel Lee."

"Oh, don't!" said Maggie, rising to her feet, her face pale as death. She put her hand to her heart as she spoke. A pang, not so much mental as physical, had gone through it.

"My dear, I think you must listen to me while I give you a message from one whom you dearly loved, whose death has changed you, Maggie, whose death we have all deeply mourned."

"A message?" said Maggie. "What message?"

"I regarded it as the effects of delirium at the time," continued Miss Heath, "and as you had fever immediately afterward, dreaded referring to the subject. Now I blame myself for not having told you sooner, for I believe that Annabel was conscious and that she had a distinct meaning in her words."

"What did she say? Please don't keep me in suspense."

"It was shortly before she died," continued Miss Heath. "The fever had run very high, and she was weak, and I could scarcely catch her words. She looked at me. You know how Annabel could look, Maggie. You know how expressive those eyes could be, how that voice could move one."

Maggie had sunk back again in her chair; her face was covered with her trembling hands.

"Annabel said," continued Miss Heath, "'Tell Maggie I am happy. I am glad she will marry…'—I think she tried to say a name, but I could not catch it—'Tell her to marry him, and that I am *very* glad.'"

A sob broke from Maggie Oliphant's lips. "You might have told me before!" she said in a choked voice.

❧XXXII❧

The Princess

he great event of the term was to take place that evening. *The Princess* was to be acted by the girls of St. Benet's, and—by the kind permission of Miss Vincent, the principal of the entire college—several visitors were invited to witness the entertainment.

The members of the Dramatic Society had taken immense pains; the rehearsals had been many, the dresses all carefully chosen, the scenery appropriate—in short, no pains had been spared to render this lovely poem of Tennyson's a dramatic success. The absence of Rosalind Merton had, for a short time, caused a little dismay among the actors. She had been cast for the part of Melissa:

> "A rosy blonde, and in a college gown
> That clad her like an April daffodilly."

But now it must be taken by someone else.

Little Ada Hardy, who was about Rosalind's height and had the real innocence which, alas!, poor Rosalind lacked, was sent for in a hurry. Carefully drilled by Constance Field and Maggie

241

Oliphant, she was sufficiently prepared to act the character by the time the night of the performance arrived.

The other actors were, of course, fully prepared to take their several parts, and a number of girls were invested in the

"Academic silks, in hue
The Lilac, with a silken hood to each,
And zoned with gold."

Nothing could have been more picturesque, and there was a buzz of hearty applause from the many spectators who crowded the galleries and front seats of the little theater when the curtain rose on the well-known garden scene. The girls walked slowly about among the orange groves and by the fountain jets. In the distance the chapel bells tolled faint and sweet. More maidens appeared, and Tennyson's lovely lines were again represented with such skill, the effect of multitude was so skillfully managed that the "six hundred maidens, clad in purest white," appeared really to fill the gardens.

The curtain fell, to rise in a few moments amid a burst of applause. The Princess herself now appeared for the first time on the little stage.

"She stood
Among her maidens, higher by the head,
Her back against a pillar."

"Perfect!" exclaimed the spectators. The interest of everyone present was more than aroused; each individual in the little theater felt, though no one could exactly tell why, that Maggie was not merely acting her part, she was living it.

Suddenly she raised her head and looked steadily at the visitors in the gallery: a wave of rosy red swept over the whiteness of her face. It was evident that she had encountered a glance that disturbed her composure.

The play proceeded bril-liantly, and now the power and originality of Priscilla's acting divided the attention of the house. Surely there never was a more impassioned Prince.

Suddenly she raised her head and looked steadily at the visitors in the gallery: a wave of rosy red swept over the whiteness of her face.

Priscilla could sing; her voice was not powerful, but it was low and rather deeply set. The well-known and familiar song with which the Prince tried to woo the Princess lost little at her hands.

O Swallow, Swallow, flying, flying South,
Fly to her, and fall upon her gilded eaves,
And tell her, tell her what I tell to thee.

O tell her, Swallow, thou that knowest each,
That bright and fierce and fickle is the South,
And dark and true and tender is the North.

Why lingereth she to clothe her heart with love,
Delaying as the tender ash delays
To clothe herself, when all the woods are green?

O tell her, brief is life but love is long,
And brief the sun of summer in the North,
And brief the moon of beauty in the South,

O Swallow, flying from the golden woods,
Fly to her, and pipe and woo her, and make her mine,
And tell her, tell her that I follow thee.

Priscilla, too, had encountered Hammond's earnest gaze. That gaze fired her heart, and she became once again not herself but he. Poor, awkward little Prissie sank out of sight; she was Hammond pleading his own cause, she was wooing Maggie for him in the words of Tennyson's Prince.

> I cannot cease to follow you, as they say
> The seal does music; who desire you more
> Than growing boys their manhood; dying lips,
> With many thousand matters left to do,
> The breath of life; O more than poor men wealth,
> Than sick men health—yours, yours, not mine—but half
> Without you; with you, whole; and of those halves
> You worthiest, and howe'er you block and bar
> Your heart with system out from mine, I hold
> That it becomes no man to nurse despair,
> But in the teeth of clench'd antagonisms
> To follow up the worthiest till he die.

In the impassioned reply that followed this address, it was noticed for the first time by the spectators that Maggie scarcely did herself justice. Her exclamation—

> I wed with thee!
> I, bound by precontract
> Your bride, your bondslave!

The rest of the play proceeded well, the Prince following up his advantage until his last words—

> Accomplish thou my manhood and thyself;
> Lay thy sweet hands in mine and trust to me,

—brought down the house with ringing applause.

The curtain fell and rose again. The Prince and Princess stood with hands clasped. The eyes of the conquered Princess looked again at the people in the gallery, but the eyes she wanted to see did not meet hers.

An hour later Maggie Oliphant had occasion to go back to the forsaken green-room to fetch a bracelet she had left there. Priscilla was standing in the corridor when she passed. Quick as lightning Prissie disappeared, and making her way into the library, which was thrown open for a general reception that evening, sought out Hammond. Taking his hand, she said abruptly:

"Maggie is in the green-room. Go to her."

He raised his brows; his eyes seemed to lighten and then grow dark. They asked Priscilla a thousand questions.

Replying to the look in his eyes, Priscilla said again, "It is cruel of you to leave her alone. Go to her. She is waiting for you—and oh, I know that her heart has been waiting for you for a long, long time."

"If I thought that . . ." said Hammond's eyes.

He turned without a word and went down the long corridor that led to the little theater.

❦XXXIII❧

Priscilla's Promise

ate that evening, after all the bustle and excitement were over and most of the guests had left, Miss Heath was standing in her own sitting room talking to Prissie.

"And you have quite made up your mind, Prissie?"

"Yes," answered Priscilla. "I heard from Aunt Ruby today; she told me all about Mr. Hammond's visit, for Mr. Hayes went to see her and told her everything."

"Well, Prissie," said Miss Heath, "what have you decided? It is a great chance for you, and there is nothing wrong in it. Indeed, this may be the direct guiding of Providence."

"But I don't think it is," said Priscilla in a slow voice. "I have thought it all over very carefully, and I don't think the chance offered by dear Maggie would be a good one for me."

"Why not, my dear? Your reasons must be strong when you say this."

"I don't know if they are strong," answered Priscilla, "but they are at least decided. My father and mother were poor and independent. Aunt Ruby is very poor and also independent. I fancy that were I rich in comparison, I might cease to be independent. The strong motive power might go. Something might be taken out of me which I could never get back, so I . . ." Her lips trembled.

"You have done everything for me, Priscilla," replied Hammond. "I shall bless you while I live."

"Pause a minute, Prissie. Remember what Maggie offers—a sufficient income to support your aunt, to educate your sisters, and to enable you to pursue those studies at St. Benet's for which you have the greatest talent. Think of the honors that lie before you; think how brilliantly you may pass your honors examination with your mind at rest."

"That's not the point," said Priscilla. There was a ring in her voice. "In a question of this kind, I ought never to content myself with looking at the brilliant and tempting side. Forgive me, Miss Heath. I may have done wrong after all; but, right or wrong, I have made my resolve. I will keep my independence."

"Then you will give up your Latin and Greek?"

"For the present, I must."

"And you are quite happy?"

"If Maggie and Mr. Hammond will only marry one another, I shall be one of the happiest girls in the world."

There came a knock at the door. Priscilla opened it.

"Prissie, darling?" said Maggie Oliphant's voice. She flung her arms round the young girl's neck and kissed her several times.

"It's all right, Priscilla," said Geoffrey Hammond.

Miss Heath made a step or two forward.

"Come and tell Miss Heath," said Prissie. "Miss Heath, here is Maggie! Here is dear Maggie and here is Mr. Hammond, and it is all right." Tears of gladness filled Priscilla's eyes. She went up to Hammond, took one of his hands in both her own, and said in a voice of rapture, "I did help you tonight, didn't I? You know I said I would do anything in the world for you."

"You have done everything for me, Priscilla," replied Hammond. "I shall bless you while I live."

Maggie Oliphant's arms were round Miss Heath's neck; her head rested against her breast. "We have come straight to you," she said. "You told me that if—if such an occasion came, you would act as a mother to me."

"So I can and so I will, dear child. God bless you. You are happy now."

"Happy!" Maggie's eyes were glistening through the softest rainbow of tears. Hammond came and took and kissed the hand which Maggie had suddenly thrown at her side.

"We both owe everything to God—and to Priscilla," he said.

❧❧❧   ❧❧❧   ❧❧❧

Before Maggie Oliphant left St. Benet's, she brought some of the honor which had long been expected from her to the dearly-loved halls; she took a first class in her honors examination. With her mind at rest, a great deal of the morbidness of her character disappeared, and her last term at St. Benet's reminded the students who had known her in Annabel Lee's time of the brilliant and happy Maggie.

Miss Oliphant's bad half hours became rarer and rarer, and Hammond laughed when she spoke to him of them and said that she could not expect him to believe in their existence.

Shortly after the conclusion of the summer term, Maggie and Hammond were married, and the little world at St. Benet's had to get on without her great presence.

By this time, however, another girl was more than filling the place left vacant by Maggie. Extreme earnestness, the sincerity of a noble purpose, and the truthfulness of a nature which could not stoop to deceit were spreading an influence on the side of all that was good and noble. No girl did more honor to the Lord above, as well as Heath Hall, than she who, at one time, was held up to derision and laughed at as odd, prudish, and uninteresting.

Priscilla's promise was evident to all. Her teachers prophesied well for the future that lay before her; her feet were set in the right direction; the aim of her life was to become not learned, but wise; not to build up a reputation, but to gain character; to put blessedness before happiness, duty before inclination.

Women like Priscilla live at the root of the true life of a worthy nation. Maggie Oliphant has brilliance, beauty, wealth; she has also strong personal influence and the power of creating love wherever she goes; but when Priscilla Peel leaves St. Benet's, she is more missed than is Maggie.

THE END

249

Victorian Bookshelf Series